▰▰▰▰ *Monday in Odessa*

THE JEWISH PUBLICATION SOCIETY
Philadelphia · New York · Jerusalem   5746-1986

Monday in Odessa

Eileen Bluestone Sherman

Copyright © 1986 by Eileen Bluestone Sherman
All rights reserved   First edition
Manufactured in the United States of America
Library of Congress Cataloging in Publication Data

Sherman, Eileen Bluestone.
  Monday in Odessa.

  Summary: Optimistic about her chances in the upcoming
all-city story-telling contest, a young Jewish girl is devastated
when her parents announce their plans to apply for a visa to
leave the Soviet Union.
  [1. Jews—Soviet Union—Fiction] I. Title.
PZ7.S54552Mo 1986   [Fic]   85–23723
ISBN 0–8276–0262–6

Designed by Adrianne Onderdonk Dudden

To Neal

Contents

1   *Round Two*   3
2   *A Heart of Courage*   16
3   *Another Story*   30
4   *A Bunny, a Beating, and a Book*   45
5   *Conversations*   58
6   *The Invitation*   73
7   *OVIR*   92
8   *Every Monday*   112
9   *Thirty Days*   135

A FINAL WORD   *163*

Monday in Odessa

1

Round Two

Slowly, the students marched to the front of the auditorium. One by one, each took a seat on stage. No one smiled. No one even dared to meet the eye of a friend in the audience. On this Monday, twelve children were about to begin Round Two of Odessa's famous eighth-grade storytelling contest, and they were scared.

Marina Birger had the unlucky position of being the last to present her story. Before taking center stage, she would have to sit still for almost an hour. Actually, this demand seemed easy compared with her other worry.

Marina was the first Jew ever to make the semifinals. Others had tried. In fact, four years earlier, Marina's cousin had been named as a semifinalist, but he was quickly disqualified when the judges realized their oversight. They made up a lame excuse about miscalculating scores. But everyone knew the truth. The Russian authorities did not want a Jew in the competition.

Yet today Marina sat on stage, and no one seemed very surprised. She had always excelled in school. Even those teachers who tried their best to belittle the Jewish pupils found it difficult to find fault with Marina. "You're such a sweet and gifted child," her sixth-grade teacher once remarked. "What a pity you're a Jew."

Marina never answered these ugly comments. She was proud and strong and certain of her own success, Jewish or not. Patiently, she waited for her moment of recognition.

Most people assumed that this was the moment, but Marina knew better. As the first presentation began, she caught a glimpse of her parents in the audience. Her husky father looked very uncomfortable in the narrow wooden seats. She wondered what he was thinking about. Marina doubted that either her father or mother was rooting for her success.

The events of the last eight weeks suddenly became vivid in her mind. She could not recall the date when Mrs. Krezshnovskaya announced the rules of the contest. "The eighteenth? The nineteenth? Oh, no matter," she thought to herself. She still remembered the excitement she felt that chilly November day.

"Mama, Papa, I've got the greatest news," said Marina as she collapsed on the worn sofa bed. She had just run up four flights of steps to her apartment. "Mrs. Krezshnovskaya explained all the rules. Round One begins in two weeks. I've got the best idea for a story."

"Slow down, Marina," ordered Klara Birger. "I didn't understand one word. Now try it again."

"And relax," added her father, Vasily Birger.

The two adults tried their best to look displeased. But they could not help but smile at their only child.

Marina returned the smile. "I'm sorry. It's just that I'm so excited."

"Well, tell us again," Vasily said. "What's so wonderful?"

"The storytelling contest. What else? I just know I've got a chance."

Mrs. Birger exchanged a worried glance with her husband. "Marina, we know you'll do a good job writing an original story and presenting it. But, please, don't ever think of it as a contest."

"I'm surprised at you," her father added, shaking his head. "You remember what happened to your Cousin Joseph. You're no different. You're a Jew."

"I know I'm Jewish, Papa. I haven't forgotten."

"And the judges don't forget either," Mrs. Birger said sharply.

Marina's eyes swelled with tears, but she was determined not to cry until she had her say. "I probably won't win. I realize it's just about impossible for a Jew to be selected as a semifinalist, but can't I try? Maybe this time will be different. I'm good. You know I'm good."

Marina was a fine actress. For years she had been turning their crowded one-room apartment into a theater, but teachers and classmates had never seen her perform. School presentations were mostly group readings or short recitations about the virtues of communism. The storytelling contest was the first time Marina had the opportunity to demonstrate her true dramatic abilities.

Mr. Birger went to hug his daughter, but Marina turned away from him. Her father looked hurt, but at the moment she didn't care. Why didn't her parents understand?

"Marina," sighed Mrs. Birger, "you know our lives are hard. It's tough enough to be Russian, let alone a Russian Jew."

"Please, Mama, not the same old lecture."

"Yes!" snapped her father. Marina knew that tone. It meant no more discussion.

"Yes, the same old lecture," Mr. Birger repeated in a calmer but still very stern voice. "Life is not easy. We are always scared—always looking over our shoulders, afraid one day we'll wake up in a labor camp."

"Sh. Not so loud," Mrs. Birger whispered. "Someone may hear you."

"I'm sorry," Mr. Birger continued quietly. "We love you, and we know you're a wonderful actress. But, darling, you're a Jew in Russia. Nothing will ever change that."

Marina nodded and let the subject pass. She knew her parents were right. Suddenly she felt very foolish. Just as her mother advised, she wrote and memorized a story. She did not even bother to mention to her parents the date of her first recitation.

Her classmates expected Marina to present a good story, but no one suspected she was such a talented storyteller. Certainly Mrs. Krezshnovskaya was not prepared for the surprise.

"Marina, please take your place on stage," Mrs. Krezshnovskaya said in her usual nasal tone. "Children, there is too much squirming in the seats. Yuri, turn around. Shura, don't pick at your nails. What a filthy habit! Remember, we're looking for self-control. A good Soviet needn't be reminded about self-discipline. I don't care how imaginative your story is or how well you present it. If you can't sit still with eyes front, we cannot consider you for Round Two."

Normally, Marina hated Mrs. Krezshnovskaya's nagging lectures. "She's a mean, dried-up prune. Everyone hates her. I almost feel sorry for the old bag of bones," she confided to her father the second week of school. But today this constant "nit-picking" was keeping Marina from thinking about the task at hand. Finally she saw the solemn nod from the back of the auditorium. Marina took a step forward and began her recitation.

At the end of her story, Marina quietly took her seat. Mrs. Krezshnovskaya and the other two judges said nothing, but Misha Pasternack, the brightest and best-looking boy in class, flashed one of his famous grins. He caught Marina's eye and nodded his head in approval. Marina had a big crush on him. At that moment she forgot about the storytelling contest entirely. All she could think of was Misha's beautiful smile.

That night Marina did not mention a word about the contest. "Why rehash the old arguments?" she thought to herself as she lay on the tiny sofa bed, listening to her father's snores. Many years later she would think of how peculiar it had been for her parents and her to play, study, eat, and sleep in one cramped room, but tonight everything seemed right. As Marina's eyes grew heavy, her final thoughts were of Misha's wonderful smile.

Suddenly everyone was laughing. Marina stopped daydreaming and turned her attention to the third storyteller. His presentation was very funny. Marina noticed that even her parents were laughing.

After all these weeks they still had not heard her story. She purposely had not volunteered to recite it for them, and they never asked to hear it. Although they tried to appear supportive, Marina knew they really wished she had not been selected. They made that quite clear the afternoon she announced her victory.

"We're very proud of you, darling. Just remember, Round Two is not until the middle of January. Something could happen like with your Cousin Joseph."

"Mama! It won't happen this time. Even Mrs. Krezshnovskaya had a nice word for me. It must have killed the old crow to say something nice."

"Please, Marina," Mrs. Birger said, "have respect for the woman! She has something to teach you, I'm sure."

"Your mother and I are thrilled about the wonderful news," Marina's father said. "I guess this is the day for good news."

Marina looked up as she started to munch on a roll. "Really?" she asked. "Why, what else has happened?"

"Look," whispered her mother as she pulled out a letter from her skirt pocket. "This is the second letter we've received from your Aunt Lena in Kansas City."

"I didn't know we had already heard from Aunt Lena and Uncle Aleksandr," Marina said between bites of the roll. "How's Joseph?"

"Don't speak with your mouth full. He's fine," her mother replied. "It was the day you rushed in here with the news of the contest. We were so involved in that, we just didn't mention it."

Marina said, "Oh, well, are they ragged, starving, and living in those creepy old buildings with rats and broken glass?"

"God forbid!" exclaimed her father. "Marina, why would you talk like that?"

"I'm only describing what I saw on film in current events. The poverty in America is sinful. You can't believe how many people have no food, no jobs, no money—nothing! It's pitiful." Marina was now picking the crumbs off the black apron of her school uniform. She really had no interest in the contents of the letter, but she suspected she would still hear all the news.

Mr. and Mrs. Birger pulled their chairs closer to their daughter's. The three sat in silence around the very small kitchen table.

When Marina swallowed her last bite, Mr. Birger began in the faintest whisper. "We have seen those films. I imagine there is some truth in them, but we think much of it is propaganda. Our family is doing well in America. I never thought I'd say this, but I think your aunt and uncle made the right choice. Yes, they have problems over there, but not like ours."

Marina had a bad feeling about this conversation, but she remained silent. Her father continued.

"Do you remember how upset I was when Aunt Lena first mentioned the subject . . . when was it . . . about two years ago? And she was still talking about

Joseph and this storytelling contest. I told her she was crazy. If they didn't end up in Siberia, they'd be miserable paupers in a strange country. I begged them to forget the idea."

"So what did Aunt Lena write?" Marina finally asked. "Are they rich, living in a mansion with thousands of servants?"

"We can do without your sarcastic remarks," Mrs. Birger said.

"I'm sorry, Mama. What did they write?"

"Well," her mother began softly, "Aunt Lena said there are groups that help you with housing, jobs, and, of course, learning the language. You're not just dropped in a slum and forgotten. Anyway, Joseph has learned English very quickly. He's attending an American high school. Your aunt and uncle are having a more difficult time with the language. But that's to be expected. It's harder for adults."

Marina really wanted to end the conversation. In her sweetest voice she said, "If they're happy, I'm happy for them. By the way, when's dinner? I'm starving!"

"You just had bread, and we are not finished," Mrs. Birger snapped.

"Please, Marina," her father gently pleaded, "we need to talk. We are very happy about your news today. It's history. Your name will be on the lips of the entire Jewish community of Odessa. Your name will also be on the lips of the rest of the Russian community.

No doubt some of their comments will not be as favorable. Some will begrudge a Jew any honor—even the semifinals of a children's contest."

Marina sat up very straight in her chair. "I don't understand," she interrupted. "Why are you talking about the contest? I thought we were discussing Aunt Lena in America."

"We are," responded her mother. "Listen, and you'll understand."

Mr. Birger began again. "Marina, the saddest part about your news is that it is very unlikely that you can be chosen for the city-wide finals. My guess is that, at least for Round One, you presented the best story, otherwise you never would have been selected as a semifinalist. But when you step onto that stage, everyone will just see you as 'the Jew.' "

"I don't care!" Marina said angrily. "I'll dazzle them again."

"Don't you understand?" her dad asked. "In the United States, Jewish citizens can achieve their goals. Here, that is not true."

"What angers me most," her mother added, "is that we are excluded and hated for a religion we never worship or study. We have been denied so long, it is only their hatred that identifies us as Jews."

Marina knew such talk sent people to labor camps. "Please, Mama, don't ever talk like that," Marina implored. "You know it could mean trouble."

Mr. Birger stood up and kissed his daughter on the

top of her head. He walked into the living room to the large red brocade sofa bed and sank down into it. He called to Marina.

Marina looked at her mother. Then she stood up and joined her father.

"Marina, it is hard, I know," whispered Mr. Birger as he stroked her flushed cheek. "Your mother and I have suspected it for a long time, but today's letter answered all our doubts. We must leave. We must start again. We plan to apply for an exit visa."

Marina was stunned. The happiest day of her life had just become a nightmare. Once a family applied for a visa, their lives were in jeopardy. The most insignificant incident could trigger a person's arrest. Worst of all, no one could predict when or even if an individual visa would be issued. Some families had been denied several times.

"No, I won't go!" cried Marina. "You can't make me. Please don't make me. Why would you do such a thing? Odessa is our home. I don't want to live anywhere else! I don't want to be the Russian foreigner! How is that any better than being the Jew in the semifinals? Besides, if you apply now, you'll ruin my chances completely. Please don't do it. The contest is important to me!" Marina kept screaming excuse after excuse, but the real excuse, the fear of losing her parents, she kept to herself. It was too painful to say aloud.

"Sweetheart, calm down," soothed Mrs. Birger as she ran from the kitchen area. No one's doing anything yet." Suddenly she took a hard look at her daughter. Marina's creamy white skin was beet red, and her green eyes were half shut. Mrs. Birger put her hand on Marina's forehead.

"You're feverish. Lie down," her mother said.

Mr. Birger stared at his child. "I never expected this response. We thought you would be excited about the decision."

"But I'm not!" Marina cried, popping up from the pillow.

"Sh, and lie down," her father stated calmly. "You get yourself well, and prepare for your important day. Afterward, we'll discuss this."

"But what if I'm chosen for the finals? You won't make me give it up, will you?"

Mr. Birger sighed. "Let's wait and see."

Marina smiled faintly. Perhaps she still had a chance. As long as she was in the contest, she knew her folks would postpone their application. More than ever she wished to prove her parents wrong. The storytelling contest was no longer a dramatic exercise. Suddenly, it marked a turning point in her life.

Marina's parents' prediction came true. Everyone was talking about her. The Jewish families were delighted. Some of the others were not so pleased. A few of her classmates made a point to repeat the anti-Semitic remarks. Even a couple of teachers had some nasty comments and treated Marina with a new coldness. These attitudes hurt the young student, but she refused to discuss her feelings at home. After all, such a discussion would just encourage her parents to apply for the visa.

The applause from the audience startled Marina. She watched the storyteller take his bow, and then realized she was next. In the last month she had imagined this moment many times. She always knew she would be nervous. Her stomach felt queasy. She was sure her lunch was coming up any moment. Her feet were numb from sitting in one position for such a long time. She thought, "If I don't throw up, my legs will probably buckle under me."

Marina almost missed her introduction. As soon as her name was spoken, however, an inner strength took control. Marina gracefully walked to center stage, made eye contact with her audience, and began.

2

A Heart of Courage

"You were sensational!" hollered Misha at the top of his lungs. He ran down the school steps trying to catch Marina's attention.

She was so involved in her own thoughts that she did not realize he was speaking to her.

"Hey, I said you were terrific." Misha's tall, lean body was now standing behind Marina. He tapped her on the shoulder, and she looked up startled.

"I'm sorry," she said softly, clutching her books to her warm beaver coat. "Were you speaking to me? I didn't mean to ignore you. It's just that I have a lot on my mind."

"Well, I guess so," teased Misha, grinning from ear to ear. "You're a celebrity. Everyone loved your story. I bet you win or at least get chosen for the city finals. You're so good, no one cares you're Jewish."

"I do!" Marina said angrily. Misha had not expected this response. He looked hurt, and Marina felt terrible. Suddenly she realized she was face to face with Misha Pasternack, and she was yelling at him. What was wrong with her? She quickly apologized.

"I'm really sorry, again. I don't know why I'm acting like this," she sighed. "I'm glad you liked it."

"Oh, I did! I did!" he proclaimed over and over again. "I'm not good at that sort of thing, but you're fabulous."

Marina loved the praise. She knew her performance had been successful, but hearing the compliments from Misha meant a lot. She hoped he was right about her making the finals.

"Do you really think it won't matter?" questioned Marina anxiously.

"What won't?" asked Misha.

"You know, about being Jewish. I hope they won't hold it against me. My parents keep telling me I don't have a chance, but I hope they're wrong. It's so important that I make it."

"Oh, it's just a contest," Misha replied casually.

"Your folks are probably right, but I still think you were the best."

Marina suddenly burst into tears. Deep inside she, too, knew her parents had always been right. She felt helpless to alter their plan to apply for an exit visa.

"Hey," he began uneasily, "I hope you win. I really do. I didn't mean to make you cry. Look, I wish I could stay and talk, but I promised my mom I would help her unpack some boxes. We moved last night." Misha felt awkward about leaving Marina, but the more he talked, the more she cried. Finally he just said, "Well, see you tomorrow."

Marina did not bother to watch Misha run across the street. If she had, she would have seen him enter her apartment building.

Finally Marina wiped her cheeks. Listlessly, she continued home. A few tears were still trickling down her face as she dragged her feet up the four flights of steps. Slowly she opened the front door.

"Marina?" cried her mother from the kitchen. "Is that you?"

"Yes, Mama." Marina placed her heavy school books on the table in the narrow foyer, and without even unbuttoning her coat, she plopped onto the soft, red sofa bed. She snuggled in her warm coat and remembered the day her mother had surprised her with it. The fur had belonged to her Aunt Lena, but with a few alterations it looked just like new. At the time, Marina thought she must be the luckiest girl in Odessa. After all, only wealthy families dressed their children in real fur coats. Today, however, she did not feel so lucky. She would gladly give up her precious fur coat if her parents would give up their plans.

Klara entered from the kitchen and proudly stared at her daughter. Finally she asked, "Darling, why are you sitting like that? You'll get overheated."

Marina took off her coat. She was completely oblivious to her mother's excitement.

"By the way, was there any talk after your performance? Did any of the teachers say anything? Your father and I were so proud. We wanted to congratulate you afterward, but we had to return to work."

"The teachers aren't allowed to say anything," answered Marina in a monotone. "But some of the kids told me they really liked it." Marina purposely did not mention her conversation with Misha. She had never told anyone about her feelings for the boy. She certainly had no intention of revealing the secret now.

Marina suddenly noticed her father's absence. Usually both parents were home when she returned from school.

"Where's Papa? Did he have to stay later to make up the missed time?"

"No, not yet," answered her mother. "We promised to go in an hour earlier tomorrow." Both Mr. and Mrs. Birger worked at the largest hospital in Odessa. She was a pharmacist. He was the assistant supervisor of medical supplies.

"Your father was so excited about your performance, he ran out to buy some special treats for supper. Let's hope for the best. The last time he felt so impulsive, he stood in line two hours for a single bottle of vodka."

Mrs. Birger chuckled as she finished her sentence, but Marina's expression did not change. She was only half-listening to her mother's chatter.

Both were startled by the booming voice from the doorway. "Is the famous storyteller here? I've got a surprise. Close your eyes."

"So soon?" asked Klara. "Well, there's no doubt about it. Today is your day, Marina. What did you get, Vasily?"

"Nothing to eat," he sighed as he walked into the living room. "Our shelves look better than the ones in the market. The stores have nothing, and the lines of people for what is left are ridiculous. Besides, we've got food in the house."

"It's okay with me. I'm not very hungry," added Marina, who had just opened her eyes. She did not see any surprise, but she didn't care. She felt horrible. Her parents seemed so excited about the contest, and still there was no mention of the visa. Why were they torturing her like this?

Suddenly a horrible thought popped into Marina's head. What if they had already applied for the papers? Marina could not stand it any longer. She needed to know their intentions.

"Papa, Mama, before you say any more, please tell

me the truth. Did you apply for the visa? Is that why you're acting so happy about my story? Please tell me. I must know."

"Marina, I don't understand you!" Klara answered. "We have never deceived you. How can you ask such a question?"

For the second time that day Marina burst into tears.

Mrs. Birger hugged and rocked her child gently. She hated seeing her daughter so unhappy. In her sweet soprano voice Klara sang a familiar lullaby.

> My child, with the thoughtful stare,
> My child, with the long, dark hair,
> My child, with skin so very fair,
> Please know for you I'll always care,
> Please know for you I'm always there.

"I'm sorry," Marina said, blowing her nose. "I know I cry too much. I act like a big baby. But I can't help it. I love you both so much, and I worry about your safety."

"Oh, Marina," began her father, "don't worry so much. Today you're a star. Sweetheart, I must admit I was doubtful, but you fooled us all. You were absolutely stunning this afternoon."

"Thank you, Papa! It wasn't so difficult. The story just came to me. I guess it was something you and Mama mention all the time. You know, about life being hard and preparing for it. In real life I'm such a chicken. I guess the theme of bravery appeals to me."

"Nonsense!" exclaimed Mrs. Birger. "You're not a coward. Look what you did today," and she hugged Marina one more time.

"Thank you! I feel much better, and I promise to be more cooperative. If you really want to go to America, it will be all right." The worried look returned to Marina's face.

"Not so fast, Marina! I think you just may have a chance for the finals, and I seriously doubt they fly contestants in from Kansas City."

"Oh, Papa, do you mean it?" Today, indeed, was her day. First, Misha congratulated her on the school steps, and now her parents were again postponing their plans.

"Please, dear, we don't want to give you false hopes," her mother cautioned, "but Papa and I think there may be a very slim possibility the judges will select you. Certainly, you deserve the honor, but, of course, that's not the question. In any case, we wouldn't do anything right now to upset your chances."

"Oh, this is all so wonderful! *Now* I feel like celebrating!"

"Good," exclaimed Vasily, who was relieved to see his daughter smiling again. I guess it's time for your surprise." Very slowly the proud father reached into his jacket pocket and pulled out a small red velvet pouch. Klara smiled when she saw the sack.

"Oh, my!" Marina gasped. Very carefully Marina pulled the drawstrings loose and placed her thumb and index finger into the pouch. She gently pulled out a gold, heart-shaped locket with a diamond chip in its center. The charm hung on a delicate chain.

"This is gorgeous, Papa!" shouted Marina as she undid the clasp and fastened the necklace around her neck. Immediately she turned to face the mirror hanging behind the larger sofa. "Oh, I love it! It looks wonderful. Where did you get it?"

"We've had it for many years," explained Klara. "It belonged to my great-aunt. Her name was Esther, and, from what I've been told, she was a very talented and beautiful woman. She designed jewelry. This locket was one of her originals. Today after the performance we thought you deserved something very special. Since your story was about a heart, it seemed perfect."

"Yes, it is. It is perfect. I'll cherish it always. I'm going to wear it every day." Then Marina asked her parents with a sheepish grin, "Are there any other jewels you wish to bestow upon a star today?"

"Marina!" scolded Mr. Birger in a playful tone. "You're impossible!"

"You know I was just teasing."

With those words the conversation ended, and Marina and her mother quickly prepared the dinner celebration. Borscht with sour cream never tasted so good. Every so often during dinner Marina would inspect her locket and smile. Mr. and Mrs. Birger were delighted to see their daughter happy and relaxed.

After dinner, Marina helped her mother wash and dry the dinner dishes and then sat at the small eating table to begin her homework. She was just about to open her math book when Mrs. Birger said, "I met a new neighbor today—a very nice Jewish woman who lives directly below us. Wouldn't it be nice to go down and welcome her to the building? I didn't ask, but perhaps she has a son or daughter your age."

"Oh, Mama, please. I don't want to go knocking on doors for friends." Marina hated meeting new people.

"It will only take a few minutes," Mr. Birger assured his daughter. "Make your mother happy, and come with us to say hello."

With a sigh, Marina dutifully marched to the front door. The adults followed her down the stairway. Marina was at the neighbors' door first and knocked softly. When there was no answer, she quickly said, "Well, I guess no one's home. We'll have to meet them another time."

As the family turned toward the staircase, the door opened and Misha Pasternack appeared. "Marina, what are you doing here?" he asked.

Marina stood in the cold hallway, speechless. "I live up-up-up-upstairs," she stuttered. She had no idea what to say to him.

Finally Marina's father took charge. "Nice to meet you, son." Mr. Birger extended his arm and shook the boy's hand firmly. "We're your upstairs neighbors. I'm Vasily Birger. This is my wife Klara. Obviously you know Marina. We thought we'd come down and say hello."

"I met your mother early this morning," Mrs. Birger explained. "But if this is a bad time, we'll visit later."

"Oh, no! We just finished dinner. The place is a mess, but come in. It will be nice to do something besides unpack boxes."

The layout of the small apartment was exactly like Marina's—the dark foyer, the compact living/sleeping area, a tiny bathroom, and the small, basic kitchen.

"How sweet of you to visit," greeted Mrs. Pasternack as she quickly tried to remove paper and boxes from her guests' path. "Please excuse the chaos. It seems endless. But I'm not complaining. Since my husband's death, we've gone from one family member to another. Just too many people. Can you imagine, we waited five years for this place?"

"Oh, please, no apologies. By the way, this is my husband, Vasily. Your first name again?"

"Ina Pasternack and my son, Misha."

"Yes, we met at the door," answered Mr. Birger. "Marina and Misha are schoolmates."

"Why, of course. Misha speaks of her quite often." With that remark, it was Misha's turn to feel embarrassed.

Fortunately, Marina did not hear the comment. Her attention was elsewhere. She had spotted an old man resting on a rocking chair at the other end of the room. His eyes were closed. Misha noticed Marina's stares, and he whispered, "That's my Uncle Mordecai. He sleeps a lot."

"Only when I'm tired, Misha," said Mordecai, and he opened his eyes. "Who's here? We have visitors already?"

"Uncle, these are the Birgers," his niece explained in a loud voice. "They live above us. Their daughter Marina is a friend of Misha's."

"A little quieter, Ina, darling. I may be nearly blind, but, thank God, my ears still work." Uncle Mordecai smiled. "Now, Misha's friend come close so I can see your face. I've heard you are quite a beauty."

Misha and Marina blushed. Slowly Marina approached the old gentleman.

"Uncle, this is the girl I spoke of this afternoon," Misha said. "She's the first Jewish student to make the second round of the storytelling contest. She was sensational. I wish you had been there."

Mr. and Mrs. Birger beamed. Marina whispered, "Thank you, Misha."

"Well, young lady," Uncle Mordecai began, "Misha hasn't stopped talking about this story. I would love to hear it." Before waiting for an answer, Uncle Mordecai ordered everyone to find a seat. Marina suddenly found herself in front of a waiting audience.

Marina did not know what to do next. She felt very silly standing in this strange living room, but she did not want to offend Misha's uncle. She did not want to do anything to upset Misha.

"Thanks for your interest," she began slowly. "Misha is very nice to even mention it, but, if you don't mind, I'd rather not perform right now."

"Come on, Marina," coaxed Misha.

"Look, if I make the finals, you'll all come to hear me. If I don't, I owe you one story."

"At least you can tell me the name of your story," Uncle Mordecai said.

"It's called 'A Heart of Courage,' " Misha called out. "It's about a prince and princess who save their father from a magician's evil spell."

"Sh!" scolded Mr. Birger playfully. "You'll ruin it for your mother and uncle. We'll all listen to it at Round Three." Vasily winked at his daughter.

"According to Misha, we shall," declared Mrs. Pasternack. "I just hope the judges give Marina a fair chance." All the adults nodded in agreement.

"Oh, well," Ina continued with a deep sigh, "let's not talk of such things tonight. You are our first guests. We must toast. Come, we'll have a drink—that is, if I can find enough glasses. Help me, Misha."

Klara and Vasily stood up and followed their hostess. Misha went to help his mother. Marina turned to follow him.

"Just a minute, young lady," Uncle Mordecai said.

"Yes?" Marina asked shyly.

"I like that title—'A Heart of Courage,'" he repeated in a thoughtful tone. "How did you think of it?"

"When you hear the story, you'll understand." Marina stood there feeling awkward.

"I'm curious," the uncle remarked. "I know a story about a queen, and that title would fit very nicely."

"Really?" asked Marina, pretending to show an interest in his comments.

"I have a good idea," Uncle Mordecai continued. "It's a little late now, but you come by tomorrow night, and I'll tell you that story. I'm a pretty good storyteller myself."

Marina did not want to return the next evening. It wasn't that she disliked Misha's uncle. She just felt uncomfortable with him. Besides, she had no interest in more stories. Her only interest was Misha, and it felt strange being in his house.

"Well, I can't promise you," she said. "I usually have a lot of homework. Especially math."

Uncle Mordecai smiled one of those wonderful Pasternack smiles. "Darling, I assure you this story is as important as learning your sums. After all, you *do* want to grow up to be a Jew with a heart of courage."

Marina just shrugged her shoulders and mumbled, "I'll try to come." She figured she could think of a good excuse before tomorrow evening.

"You go join the others now," Uncle Mordecai said. "I'm feeling a little tired."

Marina went to her father's side at the kitchen table. Every so often she and Misha would exchange smiles. Marina liked that part of the visit.

Later that evening she told her parents about Uncle Mordecai's invitation. Both her mother and father told Marina it would be impolite if she did not go and listen to the story. But they agreed the decision was hers.

When she crawled into her sofa bed that night, Marina was restless. She looked at her gold heart and thought about her Aunt Esther. She thought about living in the same building with Misha. She wondered about his strange uncle and why he had talked about being a Jew with a heart of courage. And she still thought about exit visas. Finally, Marina stopped thinking and fell asleep.

3

Another Story

The school system in Odessa was divided into a morning and an afternoon session. Marina attended public school in the afternoon.

In the mornings she studied piano at a music conservatory. The school was an added expense for Mr. and Mrs. Birger, but they believed their daughter's musical training was an important part of her education. Marina practiced every day, and she was becoming a very fine pianist.

The day after her visit with the Pasternacks, however, Marina could not concentrate at the keyboard.

She kept hitting the same wrong notes and rushing sections of the sonata. Even the steady clicking of the metronome did not help her.

Finally the instructor asked, "Are you ill? I've never heard you play so poorly."

"I'm sorry, Mrs. Horrowitz," she answered. "I don't know what's wrong with me. I guess I am sick."

Class ended early. Marina had lied to her teacher. She did know what was wrong with her. She couldn't stop thinking about Misha.

That afternoon Marina was so eager to see her classmate, she walked into school and forgot to change her shoes. Children were not allowed to wear their street shoes inside the building. They wore soft shoes that looked like bedroom slippers. Fortunately, Misha warned Marina before Mrs. Krezshnovskaya entered their classroom.

"Thanks. I'll be right back," she called as she ran to change her shoes.

Misha was standing by the classroom door when Marina returned from the hall lockers.

"Thank you again. I really would have gotten it for that," she whispered.

"It's okay. Now you owe me a favor," Misha teased.

"What do you want?" Marina giggled.

"Let me think about it," Misha replied and grinned. "I'll tell you tonight when you come to hear my uncle's story."

Marina was about to tell him she could not visit that

evening when Mrs. Krezshnovskaya walked into the classroom. As always, the teacher had a sour expression on her face. Children hated her; adults feared her. Every year on parents' night she publicly reprimanded the grownups for their sons' and daughters' poor study habits, sloppy appearance, or bad behavior. Fortunately, neither Mrs. Pasternack nor the Birgers had ever been the targets of the woman's cutting tongue. Their children were excellent students.

As soon as they saw her approach, Misha sat down and Marina walked quickly to her seat across the room. Accidentally she bumped into Shura, who sat in the desk behind her.

"Take it easy, Marina," Shura snarled. "You're going to get us into trouble."

"Sorry," mumbled Marina.

In seconds the class was quiet. Marina appeared attentive, but she was still thinking about Misha. She felt a pair of eyes staring at her. Instinctively, she looked in Misha's direction. He grinned, and they both blushed. Unfortunately, Mrs. Krezshnovskaya was watching.

"I won't have it!" screamed the prim woman. "We are here to develop our minds. Conduct your love lives outside the school building. Is that understood, ladies and gentlemen?"

"Yes, Mrs. Krezshnovskaya," the class answered in unison. Misha and Marina did not look at one another again during class. They were very thankful their names had not been mentioned.

"Hey, girls!" shouted Shura in the locker room later that afternoon. "Any bets on who the 'lovers' are in Mrs. K's class?"

"Shura, you're such a busybody!" yelled Olga from the next row of lockers. "Get your gym suit on and be quiet."

"Oh, come on. It's just in fun," Shura persisted. "Besides, I'm sure everyone is just as curious as I am. I bet anything Misha Pasternack is the loverboy."

"If he's not," screamed another classmate, "he should be. He's so handsome."

Everyone laughed. Even Marina smiled.

"Okay, so we've established the boy," Shura continued. "Confess. It's one of you!" Without any warning, the obnoxious child turned to Marina. "I know. It's Marina. It's always the quiet one."

Marina remained calm and answered in her most charming voice, "Shura! You're too much!" The giggling continued while the girls finished dressing for calisthenics.

After school Marina ran home. She didn't want to hear any more of Shura's remarks. As she trudged up the steps of the apartment house, she heard a voice call out to her.

"My goodness, we sound like a herd of elephants!" Misha shouted in a very "Mrs. Krezshnovskaya-like" voice from the fourth-floor landing.

Marina looked up, startled. She couldn't imagine what her teacher was doing at her house. When she realized it was Misha, Marina started laughing. Seconds later she remembered Mrs. Krezshnovskaya's reprimand.

"You scared me," Marina said. "You sounded just like you know who."

"Thanks. I've been working on the voice for months."

"Well, if you don't mind, I think I've heard enough from Krezshnovskaya today." Marina continued to walk to Misha's floor.

"I know exactly what you mean," he answered. Marina and Misha looked at one another and broke into a fit of laughter. Marina's eyes began to water.

"You're . . . you're," gasped Misha between laughs, "such a cry baby. You even cry when you laugh."

"I know," Marina nodded in agreement. "Please, we've got to stop. My insides are killing me."

At that moment Mrs. Pasternack appeared at the doorway. "Misha, what are you doing out here? Oh, hello, Marina."

At the sound of his mother's voice, Misha became more serious. Marina tried to stop her giggles, but she couldn't.

"Whatever it is, it must be very funny." Even Ina Pasternack chuckled. Finally Marina apologized for her behavior and started up the last flight of steps.

"Don't forget, tonight," Misha called out. "My uncle will be waiting."

"But we've got so much homework, and I have to practice my piano."

"But you owe me a favor. Remember? I'm going to tell you what it is tonight."

"Okay," sighed Marina. "I'll come as soon as I can."

Marina was furious. Her mother knew that the Pasternacks were waiting for her. "Don't be in such a rush, and let me measure your head," Mrs. Birger said, waving a tape measure in her hand. "This is the last scrap from Aunt Lena's coat. If I bungle the job, that's it. No hat."

"So what? I'll live without it," Marina groaned.

"Marina! You can drive a person crazy," her mother replied. "You've been nagging me for months about this hat. Now you're completely disinterested."

"I'm still interested. It's just that right now I'm more interested in going to the Pasternacks. They are expecting me, you know! Besides, you're the one who always talks about punctuality."

"Watch that tone, young lady," reprimanded her father. He was resting on the sofa. "Misha can wait another minute."

Marina sat and stared into space while her mother measured. The extra few minutes seemed like an hour.

"All done!" Mrs. Birger announced. Marina jumped from her seat.

"One moment, Marina," her mother said.

"Yes."

"You're a young lady. Remember your manners."

"Yes, Mother," she groaned again. Marina was about to open the door when she suddenly turned around, marched into the living room, and kissed her mother on the cheek.

"What's that for?" asked Mrs. Birger.

"I'm sorry I rushed you. By the way, don't make the hat too bulky. I don't want to look like a bear or something."

Her father laughed and said, "Marina, get out of here! You're making us nuts!"

Marina ran down the steps and knocked on Misha's door. Mrs. Pasternack opened it.

"Come in, Marina. Misha and Uncle Mordecai have been waiting for you."

When Misha heard his mother's voice, he rushed to greet his guest.

"Come on, Marina. Uncle Mordecai is all ready for you." Misha pulled her into the living room. There were still boxes stacked up against one wall, but the room no longer seemed cluttered. Even a few knick-knacks had been arranged in the china cabinet. Uncle Mordecai sat in the same rocker. He motioned for Marina to come sit near him.

As she took her seat, Marina noticed a young boy's photograph on the coffee table. Russian households usually kept their family snapshots in books. Marina stared at the framed picture.

"That's a nice picture of you, Misha," she said.

Misha chuckled. His mother smiled, but Marina noticed a sad expression in her eyes.

"What is it?" asked Marina.

"Nothing!" Uncle Mordecai assured her. "You've got a good eye. That's Misha's father. The boy looks just like him—Pasternack grin and all."

"I see what you mean," Marina agreed.

The old man in the rocker cleared his throat. "My friend, you kept me waiting this evening."

"I'm sorry," apologized Marina. "I tried my best to come down early, but . . . "

"Now, Uncle," interrupted Ina, "you know it's a woman's privilege to keep a man waiting." She smiled at Marina.

"Nonsense!" he grumbled. "That's all right for a young lad like Misha. Old men don't have the luxury."

Ina shook her head while Misha and Mordecai laughed.

"Forgive us," Misha said to Marina. "You're not used to my uncle's sense of humor. Don't worry. If anyone thinks he'll live forever, it's Uncle Mordecai."

"Please, Misha, don't talk so loudly. You'll put the evil eye on me. I'm very superstitious!" he confided to Marina. "But the boy's right. I'm a fighter. I'll never give in."

"I don't understand. Who are you fighting?" she asked.

"Oh, my dear, my dear," sighed Uncle Mordecai.

"Our lives are a constant struggle. But before I start a philosophy lesson, I believe I promised you a story. Misha, get me the paper."

"Why? You know it by heart."

"Boy, do as I say," snapped Mordecai.

Quickly Misha ran to the kitchen. He returned holding an old manuscript.

"Thank you," Mordecai said. Misha handed his uncle the yellowish pages. Marina could not see what was written on the paper.

"Well, my dear, tonight I shall tell you my story. Like you, young lady, I, too, wrote stories as a boy."

"He was eight!" Misha added proudly.

"Sh, sweetheart," whispered Mrs. Pasternack.

"Thank you, Ina, but don't shush the boy. I'm pleased he remembers so well." Mordecai turned again to Marina.

"When I was a little boy in Kiev, I loved history. I still do," boasted Uncle Mordecai. He leaned for- and whispered, "I particularly love Jewish history."

The word "Jewish" sent a chill through Marina. She remembered Uncle Mordecai's disturbing question from the last evening. She wanted to go home, but she didn't want to offend Misha.

"When I was a boy," Mordecai reminisced, "my father had me keep a daily journal. I wrote about every-thing—including the Jewish holidays. They were so special in our home." For a moment Uncle Mordecai seemed lost in memories.

"Please, Uncle Mordecai, continue," begged Misha.

"I'm sorry. Where was I?" He looked down and saw the manuscript. "Oh, yes. You see in my lap the last of it—the last of my journal. It's the story of Queen Esther."

"Esther!" Marina repeated softly. "Just like my aunt." She looked down at her locket.

"You wrote a story about a courageous heart," explained Mordecai. "Queen Esther, the Jewish queen of Persia, had such a heart. She could have remained silent, but instead, she identified herself as a Jew and saved our people."

Marina listened closely. The old man retold the story of Purim word for word as he had once written it in a childhood notebook.

In the middle of the story, Misha asked if he could continue the narration. Marina was impressed that he, too, had memorized the script. Mrs. Pasternack listened proudly.

"And so," Misha concluded, "Haman perished on the very gallows built for Esther's heroic cousin. The Jews throughout the kingdom praised their queen for her bravery. They thanked God for hearing their prayers."

"That was wonderful, Misha!" applauded Marina. "But, Uncle Mordecai, you and Misha never mentioned the cousin's name."

Uncle Mordecai chuckled, "I purposely omitted it to see if you were listening. His name was Mordecai." Marina blushed and everyone laughed.

"Well, Misha," Mrs. Pasternack declared, "besides being beautiful and smart, your classmate is also a good sport."

"Thank you, Mrs. Pasternack," Marina said, "and thank you, Uncle Mordecai, for sharing your story."

A sudden knock at the door quieted the group. Marina assumed it was her mother coming to remind her about bedtime. She was surprised to hear Mrs. Stakavitzkaya's booming voice in the foyer.

"Hello. I live across the hall. I'm Mrs. Stakavitzkaya. I've been told your name is Pasternack. Any relationship to Ari Pasternack?"

"No, I'm sorry," Mrs. Pasternack said. "But it's nice of you to stop by. Please come in. Do you know Marina Birger from upstairs?"

"Yes, I know Marina," the stout woman answered as she walked into the living room. Her eye immediately spotted the manuscript in Uncle Mordecai's lap.

Marina saw her staring at the old text and said quickly, "Misha's uncle was just showing me a story he wrote as a child."

"Story," the woman thought out loud. "That reminds me. Congratulations, Marina. Your people must be very proud. The children are buzzing your name all over the street."

"Thank you, Mrs. Stakavitzkaya. My parents *are* proud."

"Oh, I don't mean your parents," the woman chuckled. "I imagine it's quite a big deal for all you Jews. Being the first time and all that. But look at me. I'm rambling on and interrupting Marina's visit. I just wanted to do my neighborly duty. Good night, all." Mrs. Pasternack accompanied the fat woman to the front door.

"What nerve!" Mrs. Pasternack cried as she walked back into the living room.

Uncle Mordecai put his finger to his lips to quiet his niece. "Sh, Inala," he whispered. "She may have her ear at our door."

"You must be very careful around Mrs. Stakavitz-kaya," cautioned Marina. "She spies on everyone, and the police know it. No one can prove it, but some of the Jewish families in the building think she'll even make up stories to cause problems."

"I'm not afraid of that pig!" Misha announced.

"What kind of talk is that?" Mrs. Pasternack asked.

"What about her talk?" he said. "What about the way she said, 'you Jews'?"

"Misha, you must be silent. You can ruin your life." Ina had tears in her eyes.

"Life?" he asked sarcastically. "What life? A life of whispering and insults? Or maybe just a life of ignorance? Look at poor Marina. Until this evening, for all she knew Queen Esther could have been another Tolstoy character!"

"Leave me out of this, Misha," insisted Marina. She admired Misha's courage, but Mrs. Stakavitzkaya's intrusion had reminded her why she never dared to learn about Judaism.

Marina stood up and started walking toward the

foyer. "It's getting late. I better go. Thanks again."

"What do you mean?" Misha cried. "We've just begun. Now we can really talk about things."

"What things?"

"Why, Israel, of course!" Misha whispered. "Going to Jerusalem. You must think about it. Every Jew thinks about it."

Marina felt that queasy feeling in her stomach. Why was everyone so intent on applying for exit visas?

"Oh," she began slowly, "are you leaving Odessa?"

Mordecai answered. "It's a dream, my young friend. Just a dream."

"Nonsense!" Misha said. "One day the Pasternack family will live in Jerusalem. We'll live like Jews."

"Hush, Misha," his mother scolded. "This talk is upsetting everyone." Mrs. Pasternack looked into Marina's green eyes. "Please, darling, try to understand. My son is a dreamer."

"Oh, Mrs. Pasternack, you needn't apologize," Marina answered. "I'm a dreamer, too. My parents are always telling me how I must be realistic, but, like Misha, I can't help it. It's just that Misha and I don't dream the same things."

"That's because you don't know the real stories—the Jewish stories," Misha said.

"Maybe you're right," Marina agreed. She did not want to argue with him. "But I can't change that."

"I can," interrupted Uncle Mordecai.

"How?" As soon as she asked, Marina was sorry she had let the word slip out of her mouth.

"Visit us. I'll teach you," he answered.

Marina knew it was against Soviet law to study Judaism. "Thank you very much, but I won't have time," she said. "I'm busy with schoolwork and piano."

Misha snapped his fingers. "That reminds me. You owe me a favor, and I know what I want."

"What?"

"Five more visits to hear my uncle's stories."

"Misha!" scolded Mrs. Pasternack. "You're being rude!"

"It's all right," Marina sighed. "A deal is a deal." Marina never went back on her word. "I really better go now," she said nervously. "My parents are pretty strict about bedtime. Thanks again." Marina ran out of the room and up to her own apartment.

Mr. Birger met his daughter at the front door and inquired about the visit. She purposely said nothing about the Jewish history lesson.

"Yes, Papa, Uncle Mordecai's story was very interesting, and he has some others he wants to tell me," she answered him.

"That's nice," called out Mrs. Birger, who was still working on the fur hat in the living room. "We can hear all about it tomorrow. Now, please, get ready for bed."

While she was in the bathroom brushing her teeth, Marina remembered the old gossip's visit.

"By the way," spoke Marina with her mouth full of toothpaste, "when I was downstairs, Mrs. Stakavitzkaya barged into the Pasternacks' living room."

"Oh, that dreadful woman!" screeched Klara. "She gives me the shivers!"

"Now, Klara, don't get so excited," soothed Vasily. "After all, she's a lonely widow."

"Who sticks her nose into everyone's business," his wife continued. "She's also an anti-Semite!"

"So who isn't?" responded Vasily. "We live in a cruel society."

"Well, Ina should be warned. I don't trust that Stakavitzkaya woman."

"Don't worry, Mama," Marina called out from the bathroom. "I told her."

"Good!" Mr. Birger said. "Now we can drop this subject. Marina, hurry up."

As she did every school night, Marina laid out her clothes for the next morning. It was always the same drab uniform—a high-collared, long-sleeved, brown dress with a black apron. The only nice features were the white lace collar and white cuffs. Mrs. Birger sewed these on by hand. Every couple of nights, she would replace one set of collar and cuffs with a clean set. Marina held up her uniform and inspected it for wrinkles and dirt. Mrs. Krezshnovskaya was very strict about good grooming.

She kissed her parents good night and curled up in her sofa bed. Tonight she did not allow any worries to plague her.

4

A Bunny, a Beating, and a Book

Mrs. Krezshnovskaya called on Yuri to recite the poem. Every time he forgot a line, he wrinkled his nose. Marina started to giggle. Yuri looked just like the rabbit on "Just You Wait."

Marina loved that cartoon. She watched the show almost every night before dinner on the family's small black-and-white TV.

"Miss Birger, would you like to share the joke with the entire class?" asked Mrs. Krezshnovskaya. Marina stopped giggling.

"I don't find anything amusing," the teacher continued. "No one is to say a word. Yuri, you will stand at the front of the class until you have completed the recitation."

Yuri began again, but he could not remember the middle part.

Marina folded her hands at her desk and watched the clouds through the window. She wondered whether an announcement would be made today. Three weeks had passed since Round Two, and still no one had mentioned a word about the storytelling contest.

As Marina stared out the window, Shura, the girl behind her, began to mouth the poem. Yuri tried to read Shura's lips, but he couldn't.

From her seat in the back row, Mrs. Krezshnovskaya could not see the girls' faces, but she suspected that one of them was prompting Yuri.

"Young ladies!" the teacher hollered as she walked toward the two girls. "Which one of you has disobeyed my order?"

Shura acted quickly. "What do you mean, Mrs. Krezshnovskaya? I'm trying my best to sit properly." She spoke in a very innocent tone.

"Perhaps Marina has an explanation," snapped the teacher. "I don't know what's happened to you. I think this storytelling contest has gone to your head. Just tell me one thing. Must you make eyes at all the boys?"

Marina did not know what she had done to provoke Mrs. Krezshnovskaya. The teacher's remark, however, reminded her of the "love life" lecture she had received a few weeks ago. Shura remembered it, too; she started laughing.

"Don't, Shura! It's not funny. Marina should be ashamed of herself."

The bell rang. Mrs. Krezshnovskaya told Marina to remain after class. Before leaving, Shura turned to Marina, "You know, you're okay. I didn't think you had it in you."

"What do you mean?" Marina asked.

"You can stop pretending. I guessed right the first time in the locker room. It was you and Misha."

"What if it was?"

"Nothing!" said Shura with a big grin. "I think it's great!"

Mrs. Krezshnovskaya looked up from her desk. "No more chatting, girls. Marina, Mr. Fyodorov is expecting you. Please, go immediately."

"What do you think the principal wants?" Shura asked as she accompanied Marina down the hallway.

"I don't know."

"Have you done anything really bad?" Shura asked.

"Of course not!" Marina insisted. "Well, unless you include the day I smiled at Misha." Both girls giggled.

When they reached the door to the office, Shura asked, "Would you like me to wait here for you?"

"Thank you, but it's not necessary."

"Well, good luck." Shura walked toward her locker, and Marina entered the office.

Usually Miss Seordnaya, the school secretary,

greeted all students at the front desk, but the secretary had already left for the day. Marina walked to the principal's closed door. She hesitated for a moment and then knocked.

"Enter!" a voice ordered. Cautiously, Marina turned the knob and peeked in at Mr. Fyodorov.

"Come in!" the voice barked again.

Marina walked into the small, windowless room and waited to be recognized. Mr. Fyodorov continued to work at his desk.

Marina had never been inside the principal's private office. The schoolrooms she knew were clean and functional but fairly drab. Walls were white or gray. The literature classroom had some pictures of writers and poets, the geography classroom had several maps, and the science facilities had a couple of sinks and some other related equipment.

For some reason, Marina had always visualized Mr. Fyodorov's office more luxurious. She had assumed his surroundings would reflect his importance.

It didn't. The room was dark and dismal. The gray walls needed a new coat of paint. Nothing hung on them except for a portrait of Lenin.

What surprised her most, however, were Mr. Fyodorov's desk and chair. Mr. Fyodorov was obese, and the furniture was too small for him. His gruff expression as well as his size made him intimidating at school assemblies. Squeezed into this tiny chair with Lenin peeking over his shoulder, he looked funny.

"Be seated," he ordered. He still did not look up from his work.

Marina quickly took a seat. She folded her hands in her lap and waited.

Mr. Fyodorov put down his pencil, stood up, and studied Marina's face. The child modestly bowed her head and stared at her hands. She felt hot and sick in her stomach.

Finally Mr. Fyodorov spoke. "Miss Birger, you have been chosen to be a finalist in Round Three."

"What?" asked a dazed Marina.

"You are a contestant in the city-wide finals," the principal repeated. "Of course," the administrator added, clearing his throat, "this choice could jeopardize the fine reputation of our school."

Marina felt her stomach muscles tighten. "You needn't worry. I will do my very best."

Mr. Fyodorov frowned. "Miss Birger, a good Soviet should never take anything for granted." He paused and looked at the portrait of Lenin. "Now, I've checked on your family's standing," he continued. "It disturbs me that you have relatives who left the Soviet Union. In the eyes of the government, they're traitors. I certainly hope your parents haven't applied for any exit visas."

"Oh, no, sir!" Marina said quickly.

"Good!" he answered. "Mrs. Krezshnovskaya assures me you are deserving of this honor, and I value her opinion."

"Well, thank you so much. It means everything to me."

"Don't thank me yet," he replied. "You have a great challenge ahead of you. Make sure nothing gets in your way!"

Marina was about to respond when the telephone rang. Mr. Fyodorov promptly dismissed her.

As she walked out the school's main entrance, Marina looked across the street and noticed Misha and his mother leaving the apartment building. She called to them, but they did not hear her.

Marina continued down the stairs, and decided to treat herself to a candy bar. Every afternoon, street vendors sold snacks and cups of seltzer to children playing on the block.

"It's cold today," the vendor said to Marina.

"It sure is," she replied as she handed him the money. "But I don't care. I feel so good, the temperature doesn't bother me." Marina gave the vendor a big smile.

As Marina turned toward her apartment house, she bumped into a stranger. "Excuse me," Marina said. "I didn't see you." The big man ignored her. She watched him motion to another man on the street, and saw the two go into her building.

When Marina opened the front door she noticed the men talking to Mrs. Stakavitzkaya in the lobby. Marina nodded hello to the fat woman and started up the stairway. Suddenly she heard her name.

"Psst. Marina. Down here." Marina looked below and saw Shura. "My goodness," yelled Shura. "You must be in a trance. You walked right past me."

"What are you doing here?" Marina asked, running down the steps. "It's getting late. Your folks will be worried."

"Oh, I'll go home in a minute," Shura replied. "I just had to find out what happened."

Marina could feel Mrs. Stakavitzkaya's eyes watching her. She was sure the nosy woman was as anxious as Shura to hear the news. Marina motioned for Shura to step outside the building.

"Hey, before I forget," said a shivering Shura, "I saw Misha leaving the building. Very convenient."

Marina blushed. "His family moved here a few weeks ago."

"Come on. It's too cold to just stand still," chattered Shura. The girls started walking toward Shura's apartment house. "So tell me. What happened?"

With a big grin Marina shouted, "Guess!"

Shura thought out loud. "Well, you're happy, so it has to be something good. Uhm . . . is it the storytelling contest? You made the finals, didn't you?"

Marina nodded.

"Oh, congratulations!" screamed Shura. "I can't wait to tell everyone."

"Oh, no. Please don't say anything. I'm sure Mr. Fyodorov wants to be the one to make the official announcement. I probably shouldn't have told you."

"Don't worry, Marina. I understand. Look, I better get home." Shura crossed the street, and Marina ran back to her apartment house.

As she trudged up the steps, Marina could hear the opening theme song to "Just You Wait." She pictured Yuri looking like the bunny and started giggling.

Marina was not certain, but she thought she heard the television show coming from Misha's apartment. She decided he must have returned home. She walked to his door to tell him to turn down the volume. Mrs. Stakavitzkaya was always complaining about things like that.

The apartment door was not completely shut. Marina felt odd barging into the Pasternacks' living room, but she did not want to scream from the hallway.

She entered and looked around the room in horror. Broken china and glass were all over the floor. The sofas had been slashed, and torn books were scattered everywhere.

Marina shut off the television and turned toward the door. Suddenly she spotted a body behind a sofa. It was Uncle Mordecai. She went right to him. His face was all bloody. He was mumbling something, but his eyes were closed. Quickly Marina took off her fur coat and covered him with it. She used her hat as a pillow.

"Don't try to move, Uncle Mordecai. I'll get help." She ran out of the apartment yelling for her parents.

Mr. Birger heard his daughter's voice. "What is it?" he screamed from upstairs.

"Please hurry. It's Uncle Mordecai. He's hurt." The Birgers quickly followed Marina into the apartment.

"Call an ambulance, Vasily."

Mr. Birger accompanied Uncle Mordecai to the hospital. Marina and her mother remained in the lobby. They waited for Misha and Mrs. Pasternack to return home.

Some of the residents were discussing the incident. "There's nothing to discuss," Mrs. Stakavitzkaya stated bluntly. "It's obvious it was the work of the authorities. Did you look at that place? They were searching for something. These Jews will never learn."

Mrs. Birger overheard the comment. "Let's not stand here," she whispered to Marina. "We should help clean up some of the mess."

Inside the apartment, Mrs. Birger kept repeating, "Perhaps they were hiding something."

Marina did not answer, but as she stacked the torn books in a corner of the room, she wondered about the "Queen Esther" manuscript. She was picking up a large anthology of fairy tales when Misha and Mrs. Pasternack appeared.

"Oh, no!" Ina cried, staring at the room. "Uncle Mordecai? Where is Uncle Mordecai?"

"Ina, calm yourself," Klara said gently. "Vasily has gone with him to the hospital."

"We must go," Misha said, and he led his mother to the door.

"Wait!" Klara said. "We'll go with you. Marina, go

get my coat." When Marina got to her apartment, she realized she still had the anthology in her arms. She tossed it onto the sofa bed and grabbed her mother's coat.

Mr. Birger greeted them at the hospital's emergency entrance. He took Ina's and Misha's hands and spoke reassuringly.

"Your Uncle is resting comfortably. I know the doctor who is caring for him. He's a fine physician."

"Thank God he's alive," Ina sobbed.

Mr. Birger stayed with the Pasternacks. Marina also wanted to stay at the hospital, but her father insisted she return home.

"Are you hungry, Marina?" asked Mrs. Birger as they walked out the hospital doors. "We never had dinner."

Marina nodded. "I'm a little hungry, Mama."

They were almost home when Marina's mother asked, "Why were you late today?" In all the confusion, Marina had not told her parents about the storytelling contest.

"I was on my way up when this whole thing happened."

"Well, why were you late?"

"I had to see Mr. Fyodorov after school."

"Are you in trouble?"

"No!" giggled Marina. "Just the opposite. They chose me for Round Three."

"Really?"

Marina nodded with a big smile on her face.

"Oh, darling, I'm so proud of you." Mrs. Birger stopped walking and hugged her daughter.

"Thank you, Mama. It is exciting."

"It's unbelievable!"

"Please, Mama," Marina began, "if I should be asleep when Papa comes home, don't spoil my surprise. I want to tell him myself."

Mrs. Birger laughed. "Of course. Now tell me everything. Exactly what did Mr. Fyodorov say?"

"Just that Mrs. Krezshnovskaya assured him I was deserving of the honor," answered Marina. She didn't mention the part about the exit visas.

When they entered the apartment, Mrs. Birger noticed the large book of fairy tales on the sofa. "Is that from school?" she asked, pointing to the anthology.

"Oh, no," Marina replied. "It's from downstairs. I brought it up by mistake."

While her mother warmed up a pot of soup in the kitchen, Marina sat on her sofa bed and read the anthology's table of contents. She turned to page 88, expecting to find one of her favorite fairy tales. She found, instead, the first page of the "Queen Esther" story. Someone had taped the old manuscript to pages 88 through 95.

"Dinner's ready," her mother called out.

Quickly Marina shut the book. She put it in a small

chest by her sofa where she kept all her schoolbooks
and papers. Then she joined her mother at the kitchen
table for a bowl of hot soup.

There was a knock at the door. "I'll get it. You eat,
Marina." Mrs. Birger got up and opened the front door.

"Is this the Birger residence?" a gruff voice asked as
two men entered the apartment.

Mrs. Birger nodded. Marina looked up and immediately recognized the taller of the two. She had seen him
talking to Mrs. Stakavitzkaya in the afternoon. He was
the same one she had bumped into on the street.

"We had a complaint about you," the shorter one
began. "What were you doing snooping around downstairs?"

"We were trying to help," Mrs. Birger answered.

"Did you find anything your government should
know about?"

"No, sir."

"We'll look for ourselves." The two men searched in
all the kitchen drawers and cabinets, the book case, and
the sofas. Then they opened Marina's small chest.

"Whose are those?" The taller man pointed to Marina's schoolbooks.

"They're mine. I'm in eighth grade."

Eighth grade?" he repeated as he picked up the book
of fairy tales. "Is Fyodorov your principal?"

Marina nodded.

The tall man flipped through the book without really
looking at the pages. Then he threw it back into the

chest. He turned to Mrs. Birger. "Do yourself a favor. Don't get involved in other people's business. Come on," he said to his partner. "Let's get out of here."

Mrs. Birger returned to her seat at the table. She stared at her cold soup and clenched her hands in her lap. Her whole body was shaking. "I hope your father comes home soon."

"It's all right, Mama. They believed us."

"Why shouldn't they?" she asked. "It's the truth."

"Of course," Marina replied. She did not mention the anthology.

5

Conversations

Marina was sleeping when her father returned from the hospital. She woke up early the next morning and tiptoed over to his side of the sofa bed.

"Please, Marina," groaned Mr. Birger. "Let me sleep a little longer."

"But, Papa," she whispered, "this is important."

"What is it?"

"I made the finals."

"That's nice," he yawned. A second later he jumped up and turned to his wife. "Klara, wake up! Wake up!"

Klara sat up startled. "What is it?"

"It's Marina. She's a finalist in the contest."

Marina started to laugh.

"What's the joke?" her father asked.

"Mama already knows. I told her last night, but she promised to keep it a secret. I wanted to tell you myself."

Marina then told her father all about the meeting with Mr. Fyodorov. She ended by saying, "I just hope Uncle Mordecai will be well enough to come to the finals. Do you remember, we all joked about it the first time we visited the Pasternacks?"

"Of course," answered her mother with a big smile. "But, Marina, don't expect too much from Uncle Mordecai. He's an old man. It will take him a long time to recuperate."

The sight of Uncle Mordecai's bloody face flashed in front of Marina's eyes. Then she remembered the knock at her own door.

"Mama, did you tell Papa about the two men?"

Her mother nodded.

"It was very frightening, Papa."

Mr. Birger hugged his daughter. "Try not to think about it," he said. "We haven't done anything wrong. Just be careful."

On their way out, Mrs. Birger reminded Marina that they would meet her after school to go grocery shopping.

"Misha wasn't in school today," Marina told her parents as they walked to the grocery store. "Is it because of Uncle Mordecai?"

"I don't know," replied Mr. Birger. "He's still in the intensive care unit. No one but family is allowed to visit."

"When it's permitted, may I go see him?"

"Of course," answered Mrs. Birger. "We'll all visit. But no more cleaning other people's apartments."

Marina suddenly turned around to see if anyone was behind them. Mr. Birger put his arm around her. "Don't worry," he whispered. "Those men only wanted to scare you."

"And Uncle Mordecai?" she asked. "Was that a scare?"

"Stop dawdling, you two!" Mrs. Birger yelled from the corner. Just then a gust of wind hit her in the face. "It's cold out here!"

Once inside the store, Mrs. Birger started grabbing items off the shelves.

"Mother," Marina said, "we have plenty of soap at home."

"Sh!" Mrs. Birger scolded as she picked up two more bars. "You've got to overbuy. After today they may not have soap for weeks. You know that."

"Okay, don't get upset. I'll stand in line for the cheese. You and Papa can meet me there."

Marina was the fourth person to take her place in line. By the time she was second, twelve people were standing behind her. The man in front of her was still placing his order when Mrs. Stakavitzkaya entered the store. She saw Marina and walked up to her.

"Be a dear, Marina. I'm in a big hurry. Let me have your spot."

"But I've been waiting, Mrs. Stakavitzkaya."

The old gossip shook her head. "I'm amazed," she said in her booming voice. "I always thought you were mannerly. Not like the other Jewish children in our building."

Marina was sure everyone in line had heard and was staring at her. "Here, take my place," she mumbled, and walked to the back of the line.

A few moments later, Mr. Birger joined his daughter. "It looks like we've got quite a wait. He folded his arms and heaved a sigh of disgust. "I just don't understand why everything must be such an ordeal. When I looked over here before, it didn't even seem like a lot of people."

"Please, Papa," Marina whispered. "I lost my place. I'll talk to you about it at home."

While Mr. Birger and Marina waited to order the cheese, Mrs. Birger was on the other side of the store in the fish line. After twenty-five minutes, she stepped up to the counter.

"Where's your paper to wrap the fish?" the man barked.

"Just a moment, sir." Mrs. Birger reached inside her cloth shopping tote for a piece of old newspaper. She always carried some. But as she reached into her bag, Mrs. Birger remembered she had used her last piece a few days ago.

"Sorry, lady. You know you've got to provide paper and shopping bags. Next, please."

Mrs. Birger quickly looked around to see if anyone could help her. An elderly gentleman handed her a sheet, but it was too late. The man behind the counter was already waiting on the next customer. Mrs. Birger was furious as she met her family at the checkout counter.

"It doesn't matter, honey," Mr. Birger consoled his wife. "We can make do. Let's go."

On their way home Mrs. Birger kept apologizing for being so careless, but Marina was not paying any attention to her mother. She was thinking about the incident with Mrs. Stakavitzkaya.

As he unlocked the apartment door, Mr. Birger remembered Marina had been very upset in the store. "What happened that you lost your place in line?" he asked.

"It's that Mrs. Stakavitzkaya! She's a witch!" yelled Marina as she threw her coat on the kitchen table.

"Marina! Hang up your coat, and don't be so fresh!"

"But, Papa, the woman forced me to give her my place in line. I hate her!"

"How did she force you?" asked Mrs. Birger, who had begun slicing the cheese at the kitchen counter.

"It was almost my turn, and she asked me for my spot. When I refused, she made this comment about me being unmannerly like the other Jewish children. Everyone was watching us. I thought I would die."

"I'm not surprised," Mrs. Birger said without look-ing up from the cutting board. "Last night she was unbelievable."

Marina sat down next to her father at the kitchen table. "Papa, I can't prove it, but I think Mrs. Stakavitz-kaya had something to do with Uncle Mordecai getting hurt."

"You have no reason to believe that," her father said. He knew Marina had a vivid imagination, but he would not tolerate wild accusations.

"I know she spoke to that same tall man who was here last night."

"What?" asked Klara. She stopped cutting and turned toward Marina.

"I saw them talking in the lobby yesterday after-noon."

Mrs. Birger put her knife down on the cutting board and walked toward her husband. "Marina is right. That woman makes up stories. They must pay her."

"Sure," Marina added. "She couldn't wait to tell them that we had gone to the Pasternacks' apartment. How else would they have known?"

Mr. Birger was quiet for a while. Then he spoke softly. "You may be right. But please forget about it. If that woman is an informer, we must be careful. Don't talk about her. Don't even think about her."

Just then they heard a knock. Marina and her mother exchanged fearful glances. The sound reminded them of last night's investigation.

"Who's there?" Mr. Birger called out.

"It's Misha Pasternack, sir. May I come in?"

Marina ran to open the door.

"Sorry to disturb you," the boy said as he followed the Birgers into their living room. "We just returned from the hospital. My mom's resting, but she wanted me to thank you for all your help."

"That's quite all right," replied Mr. Birger. "How's your uncle?" He motioned for Misha to sit down next to him. Marina and her mother sat down on the smaller sofa bed.

"They beat him up pretty bad. We hope he'll be out of intensive care by tomorrow afternoon."

"We'll visit, then." Marina tried to sound cheerful. "Will you be in school tomorrow? Do you want the homework?"

"I don't know. Our place is such a mess, and I've got to help my mom."

"Did they take anything?" Mrs. Birger asked.

Misha hesitated. "I'm not sure. I can't find one book. It's a book of fairy tales."

Marina jumped up and opened the chest where she had hidden the anthology. "I'm sorry," she said sheepishly. "I brought it up by mistake." She handed the book to Misha.

"Did you read any of it?"

Marina giggled. "I liked the story on page 88 the best."

Misha nodded and grinned. "This book means a lot

to me. It was a present from my dad." Marina was surprised to hear Misha mention his father. He seldom talked about him.

"Your mother once said he was a writer," Mr. Birger remarked.

"Yes."

"That's a wonderful job," Marina added. "I might be a writer, if I'm not an actress."

"Stick to acting. Writing can get you killed."

"What do you mean?" Marina asked, horrified.

"No one knows what happened, but my father was working on a story, and one night he disappeared."

"Do you mean they put him in a labor camp?"

"I wish they had. He still might be alive." Misha's voice started to quiver.

"You don't have to talk about it," Mrs. Birger said gently.

Misha cleared his throat. "I'm not ashamed. You see, last night was not the first time for us. When I was six and a half, my mom and I found our apartment the same way. We couldn't find my dad. Then the police came to our house and told us he had been killed— stabbed to death. They never found who did it."

Misha stood up and looked at the book in his arms. "I don't remember much about him, but I can still hear his voice reading me these fairy tales. It's funny what sticks in your mind." Suddenly the boy felt very uncomfortable. "I'm sorry for keeping you. Thanks again for all your help."

Misha left, and the Birgers returned to the kitchen for dinner. Marina remarked how sad Misha must be without a father. Mr. Birger added that they should try to help the family whenever possible. No one mentioned it, but all three were thinking the same thing—how terrifying it would be for one of them to suddenly disappear.

They were in the middle of their dinner when Marina asked, "Mama, Papa, do you ever think about living in Israel?"

"I'm surprised you ask such a question," Mr. Birger replied. "You carried on so when we talked about an exit visa."

Marina hesitated but then said, "Misha talks about Israel a lot. Of course," she added quickly, "his family has a good reason to leave Odessa."

"So do we," Mrs. Birger said emphatically. "But, if we go anywhere, we'll join Lena in Kansas City." All of a sudden, Mrs. Birger began to cry. "I can't imagine that I'll ever see my sister again."

Marina had not expected her mother to become so emotional. "I'm sorry, Mama," she said. "Are you angry with me?"

"Of course not. Why would I be?"

"If I hadn't made such a fuss, we might already be in Kansas City."

Mrs. Birger wiped her tears. "I doubt it could ever happen that quickly. Besides, we promised you a chance to be in the storytelling contest. You know I never go back on my word."

Marina did not say any more as she finished her dinner, but she could not stop thinking about her mother and aunt. Marina had always thought her mother was very lucky to have a younger sister. When she was four, Marina begged her parents to buy a baby at the hospital.

"That's one item I could get without standing in line," Klara Birger had boasted, "but, sweetheart, we don't even have enough room here for the three of us."

When Marina grew older, she realized most Russian couples had to limit their families to one child. Apartments were too scarce and too small. Still, she always dreamed about a sister. That night, Marina imagined what it must be like to lose one.

Marina was walking up the school steps when Misha sneaked up behind her.

"Boo!" he shouted.

The girl jumped. She turned around and saw Misha laughing.

"Ha, ha," she said sarcastically. "That's not very nice."

"But it's funny."

"I'm glad to see you're in such good spirits. Uncle Mordecai must be better."

At the mention of his uncle's name, Misha became

serious. "He's out of intensive care. I hope he can come home soon."

"Me, too. But please," cautioned Marina, "be more careful."

"What do you mean?"

"You know."

"No, I don't." Misha did not like Marina's insinuations. He started up the steps.

"Hey," Marina called after him. "Don't get mad. I'm trying to help."

He stopped and waited for her to catch up with him. "What do you want, Marina?"

"My father said I shouldn't talk about it," she whispered, "but you've got to know. Be especially careful in front of Mrs. Stakavitzkaya. Don't get her mad. She knows the man who searched our house."

"Your house? When?"

"The same night they beat up your uncle. I think Mrs. Stakavitzkaya made up some story."

"I don't understand," Misha said. "Why did they bother you?"

"Because they heard we had been in your apartment. My father said they were trying to scare us."

Suddenly Misha made a gesture for Marina to be quiet. She turned around and saw Mrs. Krezshnovskaya walking toward her.

"I missed you in class yesterday, Misha," she said in her annoying nasal voice. "As soon as you change your shoes, please report to my room. You have make-up work."

"Yes, Mrs. Krezshnovskaya," Misha answered politely. "I'll be right in."

She then looked at Marina. "I trust you're practicing every night. We're giving you a great opportunity."

"I know, Mrs. Krezshnovskaya. Thank you very much for recommending me." The teacher turned abruptly and walked up the steps.

Misha nudged Marina. "What did she mean?"

"Hardly anyone knows," Marina whispered, "but they chose me as a finalist for the storytelling contest."

On hearing the news, Misha threw his arms around Marina. "Why didn't you tell me?" he asked. Then he realized he was hugging a girl and immediately dropped his arms.

Marina's face was as red as his. "Sh. Don't talk so loud," she said, trying to hide her embarrassment. "I guess Mr. Fyodorov will make the announcement soon."

"Your folks must be so excited."

"They are," Marina answered. "But, to tell you the truth, with everything else that's happened, I haven't been thinking about the contest very much." Marina paused and looked embarrassed. "You'll never believe it, but after you left last night, I asked my parents about moving to Israel."

Misha flashed one of his famous grins. "Uncle Mordecai will be happy to hear that. I guess our lessons did you some good."

"Our?" Marina laughed. "You better stop congratulating yourself and get up to Mrs. Krezshnovskaya."

"I'll race you," Misha yelled as he ran up the steps. Marina tried to catch him, but he was through the doors before she reached the top step.

Later in the afternoon, Mr. Fyodorov made the official announcement at an assembly, and after the last bell everyone wanted to congratulate the winner. Marina finally made her way down the school steps when she realized her assignment pad was still in Mrs. Krezshnovskaya's room. She ran back into the school, changed into her soft slippers, and rushed down the empty corridor. The classroom door was wide open, and she could hear her science teacher speaking to Mrs. Krezshnovskaya. She did not want to interrupt them and waited in the hallway.

"Stupid! Stupid! Stupid!" Mr. Shatz kept repeating. "How could you persuade Fyodorov to pick her?"

"Our school has never won the championship," Mrs. Krezshnovskaya answered calmly. "She'll win it for us."

"Never."

"But if she's the best?"

"It won't happen," he declared. "She's a Jew."

"You surprise me. I thought you were part Jewish."

"That's why I feel this way," he snapped.

Mrs. Krezshnovskaya shook her head. "I don't understand."

"I'm more sensitive to the issue," he yelled. "What if they do something to embarrass us? What if her family applies for an exit visa? It won't look very good that you sent the daughter of 'Jewish traitors' to a prestigious contest. The authorities won't leave us alone. Besides, it's just going to give everyone another reason to hate Jews."

"You're too emotional," Mrs. Krezshnovskaya replied. "Mr. Fyodorov isn't stupid. He checked. The Birgers have never applied for a visa. Certainly, they won't now."

"Perhaps," Mr. Shatz conceded.

"Of course," Mrs. Krezshnovskaya said. "If she wins, she'll be a celebrity in Odessa. Why would her family want to leave?"

"If she wins," the science teacher corrected, "they'll never let her leave."

After listening to the conversation, Marina did not have the nerve to ask for her assignment pad. She turned around and went back to her locker. How stupid of her never to have considered the consequences of becoming known in Odessa. Mr. Shatz was right. Her family would be denied exit visas and made to suffer the rest of their lives.

When Marina reached her locker, she jerked open

the door, threw her snow boots on the floor, kicked off her slippers, and slammed the locker shut. Mr. Fyodorov heard the banging.

"Marina! Must you be so clumsy?" he shouted.

The voice startled her. "I'm sorry, Mr. Fyodorov."

"I hope so, and I hope I haven't made a mistake." He drew closer and whispered, "There will be great penalties if I have."

Marina was too scared to say anything, but the obese principal stood and waited for some type of acknowledgment. She finally nodded.

"Good! Now, put on your boots, and go home," he ordered.

Marina did not budge until she saw the principal disappear into the school office. Quickly she shoved her feet into her boots, picked up her school books, and ran to the front door. The moment she stepped outside, Marina started crying.

6
The Invitation

"This won't take long," the hospital administrator assured the Birgers as they walked into his office.

"We don't mean to rush you," Mrs. Birger explained politely, "but our daughter, Marina, will be coming home from school shortly. We like to be there to greet her."

"I understand. I'll be as brief as possible. Please sit down." Vasily and Klara sat down and faced their boss, Mr. Anatassy. The three had worked together for almost eleven years.

"Vasily, I understand you came in with a patient the other night," the administrator began. Mrs. Birger looked at her husband.

"That's right. Mordecai Pasternack."

"Is he a relative?"

"No."

"How do you know him?" asked Mr. Anatassy.

"He lives in our building," Mrs. Birger quickly replied. "His nephew Misha and our daughter Marina are friends from school."

"Is there anything wrong?" Mr. Birger asked.

The administrator leaned back in his seat and sighed. "I hope not. Two men were here this afternoon, asking about you and this Pasternack patient."

Mrs. Birger began to fidget with her wedding band. "What did you tell them?" she asked nervously.

"What I would tell anyone, Klara. That we've worked together for many years, and you're both outstanding members of my staff."

"Thank you," she whispered.

"But, if I were you two," Mr. Anatassy continued, "I'd stay away from this old man and his family."

"Why?" demanded Mr. Birger. "They're fine people." Vasily could feel the muscles in the back of his neck tighten.

Mr. Anatassy remained calm. "I don't know, Vasily. These men say they received phone calls. Someone claims the uncle was conducting religious meetings for Jews in your building."

"That's nonsense."

Mrs. Birger sat forward on her chair and said softly, "There's an old gossip in our apartment house. She makes trouble for all the neighbors. It's all lies."

"Perhaps, Klara," the administrator agreed, "but, Comrades, this man and his family are being watched. Anyone who associates with them could find themselves in serious trouble." He hesitated and then added, "Especially a Jew."

Mr. Birger clenched his fists in his lap in an effort to control his temper. "You know very well that Klara and I are law-abiding. We don't practice any religion."

"Vasily," the administrator said patiently, "don't be offended. I'm not accusing you. I'm trying to help you."

Mr. Birger knew it was pointless to continue the conversation. He stood up and extended his hand. "I didn't mean to be rude," he apologized as he and Mr. Anatassy shook hands. "I know your intentions are good. We appreciate the advice."

As they left the office, Mr. Birger leaned toward his wife. "We won't discuss this now," he whispered. They hurried home. Like her daughter the day before, Mrs. Birger kept turning around to see if men were following them.

"Stop it, Klara," Mr. Birger finally said. "If men are watching, there's absolutely nothing we can do."

As soon as they were inside their apartment, Mr. and

Mrs. Birger embraced. "I'm scared," Klara weeped into her husband's shoulder.

"I know, darling," Mr. Birger replied, "but we must not alarm Marina."

"Well, she can't keep running down to Misha's, and certainly none of us can visit Uncle Mordecai. How will you explain that?"

Mr. Birger heaved a deep sigh as he sat down on the brocade sofa. "We'll simply tell her the Pasternacks are under surveillance, and Mr. Anatassy has told all hospital employees to stay away. Meanwhile, we must prepare."

"For what, darling?"

"After the finals, we're definitely applying for the visas."

Mrs. Birger stared at her husband. "Really?" she whispered.

"Yes!"

Mrs. Birger's eyes began to swell with tears of joy. "This news is wonderful. I've wanted to hear you say those words for such a long time. I know you've had your doubts. And, of course, Marina has made it more difficult. But it's the right decision. I know it!" Klara wiped her wet cheeks and sat down next to her husband. She took his hand and squeezed it. "It's a new beginning for us."

But Mr. Birger jerked his hand away from his wife and shook his head. "Don't be so happy, Klara. It's a very big risk. We could end up as outcasts for the rest of our lives . . ." He paused and added, ". . . or something even worse."

"You're talking foolish like Marina. Lena and Aleksandr got out. More Jews are leaving every month. Why should they punish us?" Klara took her husband's hand again and squeezed it even tighter. Then she went into the kitchen to prepare dinner. Vasily pulled off his boots and sprawled out on the sofa for a short nap.

Klara stood in the tiny kitchen and stared at the high cupboard above her stove. It was the cabinet in which she kept her good china. The set of dishes had belonged to her great-grandmother, and Klara had always cherished the plates. In the last few months, however, the china had become a hiding place for a very important piece of paper. The night the men searched the house, she had been terrified that they would find the document and take it. Luckily, they had shown little interest in a set of red and gold flowered dinner dishes.

Suddenly, she had this horrible sensation that the paper was missing. Immediately she pulled open the cupboard door, and standing on her toes, began emptying the shelves. Finally, she could reach the two platters. Stretching with both arms, she pulled the first platter forward and groped for the paper behind it.

The rattling of dishes disturbed Vasily. He awoke with a start and rushed into the kitchen. He could see his wife reaching for something.

"Why didn't you call me, darling? That's too high for you."

Klara turned around holding the document. "I'm sorry I disturbed you. I was worried something had happened to this."

Mr. Birger looked at the piece of paper in his wife's hand and smiled. "You were smart to have Lena take care of that when she arrived in Kansas City. I remember I protested, but you were right."

"No apologies. I'm just happy we have it. We'll show it to Marina tonight." Mrs. Birger turned around and put the paper behind the platter again. Mr. Birger helped his wife restack the dishes.

After he closed the cabinet, Vasily looked at his watch. "Marina should be home by now." He walked over to the front window and smiled when he saw his daughter crossing the street.

But it took Marina an extra ten minutes to get up to her apartment. Just as she was coming into the lobby, she looked up and saw Misha running down the steps.

"You're getting home kind of late," he remarked as he walked over to her. Then he noticed her tears. "Hey, what's wrong?"

"Nothing," she lied. "The wind just irritated my eyes."

"Oh. So why are you so late?"

"It's a long story. I don't want to go into it." Again she started sobbing. "I'm sorry. Can I borrow your assignment pad? I left mine at school."

"Don't cry. Of course you can use mine. Hurry up, and I'll give it to you now before I go to the hospital."

Misha turned around and darted up the stairway. Marina did not have the energy to keep up with him. Finally she was at the opened door.

"Come on in," Misha called as he rummaged through his bookbag for the assignment pad. "I'll wait a few minutes, so you can copy the assignments."

Marina entered the foyer and suddenly thought of Uncle Mordecai's beating. "Please, Misha," she whined, "my folks are going to be worried, and they'll yell at me for being so late. Just give me the pad, and when you come home tonight, come get it."

"Fine," said Misha, and he handed her the assignment book. "I've got to hurry, too. My mom's waiting at the hospital." He switched the lights off, and they walked out into the hallway. As he shut the front door, he asked, "By the way, when are you coming to the hospital?"

Marina shrugged. "Depends on my folks. In a day or so, I'm sure."

"Great!" Misha flashed one of his beautiful smiles. "Well, I'll see you later."

Misha ran down the steps, and Marina turned to start up the last flight. She looked up and saw her father standing at the top landing.

"What are you doing?" he asked. "Your mother and I have been waiting for you."

"Here I come," she groaned.

Mrs. Birger greeted Marina at the door. "We were worried about you."

"That was silly. I was only talking to Misha. I had to borrow something for school." Mrs. Birger glanced over at her husband.

"Marina," ordered Mr. Birger, "hang up your coat, and come sit down."

"What's wrong?"

"Please, sweetheart. Just do as your father asks." Seconds later Marina was at her father's side.

"You are not to go into the Pasternacks' apartment again," he whispered.

"Why not?"

"And Misha shouldn't visit us," he continued softly.

"What?"

"Most important, you are not to visit Uncle Mordecai."

"But, Papa, I already told Misha we would."

"We're not permitted," interrupted Mrs. Birger.

"Yes, we are. He's out of intensive care."

Mr. Birger shook his head slowly. "Mr. Anatassy has ordered all hospital employees to avoid contact with the Pasternack family. As you already know, the family is under surveillance. Mr. Anatassy doesn't want any trouble from the authorities."

"But Misha's my friend. I can't just ignore him," cried Marina.

"You must if you want us to be safe."

Marina looked down at the coffee table and saw her books. On top was Misha's assignment pad. "He'll be here later to get his book," she said defiantly.

"This must be the last time," Mr. Birger replied.

"We can't afford any problems."

Mrs. Birger stroked her daughter's long hair. "Don't be sad, Marina. These last few days have finally given us the courage we needed months ago."

Marina jerked away from her mother's touch. "Did you do it? Did you apply?" she demanded.

Her father stood up and answered, "The day after your contest we will go to OVIR."

"No!"

"You are a child. You cannot make this decision." Mr. Birger spoke very sternly.

"But, Papa," pleaded Marina. "You're wrong. You cannot wait until after the contest. I heard Mr. Shatz say that if I win, we would never be granted visas."

"She's right, Vasily," cried Mrs. Birger. "We can't wait." For a few seconds no one said anything. Then Mrs. Birger turned to her daughter. "I have never broken a promise in my life, but now I must."

Marina shrugged. "I only wanted to win to make you give up this visa idea. I was scared something horrible might happen."

"And now?" her father asked.

"I'm still scared, but I'd feel guilty the rest of my life if I thought it were my fault that Mama never saw Aunt Lena again."

"You mustn't worry," Mrs. Birger said and gave her daughter a big hug. The mother was very touched that Marina was so concerned. "Your father and I will be just fine. Tomorrow he will go to OVIR."

"So soon?" gasped Marina.

"Of course, honey. There's no reason to wait."

"What do you do? Just fill out an application?"

Mrs. Birger chuckled. "I wish it were that simple."

"Luckily your mother took care of the first step," and Mr. Birger motioned for them all to go into the kitchen. He opened up the cabinet and pointed. "In here your mother has been hiding an invitation from Israel."

"Israel! I thought Mama would only move to Kansas City."

"Sh!" scolded Mrs. Birger. "You must never, ever say that. As far as the authorities are concerned, we are going to Israel."

Mr. Birger explained how the Soviets would only grant visas to Jews who wished to live in Israel. Every Jew had to present an official invitation from the Israeli government.

"But how did they know to mail us one? Had you written them?"

Mr. Birger looked sheepishly at his wife. "Your mother was smart enough to tell Aunt Lena to contact someone in Jerusalem. It was done as soon as Aunt Lena arrived in Kansas City."

Marina pulled out a kitchen chair and sat down. Everything was happening too quickly. "May I see it?" she asked hesitantly.

Once again the Birgers emptied the cupboard and took out the document. The three studied the piece of paper. On it were Marina's parents' and grandparents' names, as well as their dates and places of birth. At the bottom of the list Marina saw her own name.

"Can't I please tell Misha?"

"Definitely not!" yelled her father. "No one must know—for their safety and ours." He picked up the invitation and slipped it between the two platters in the cupboard. A knock at the door startled all three of them.

"It's too soon to be Misha," whispered Marina. Mr. Birger went to the front door and opened it slightly.

"Hello, Comrade Birger." Marina and her mother recognized the booming voice.

"Good evening, Mrs. Stakavitzkaya," Mr. Birger answered politely. "What can I do for you?"

"May I come in?" The nosy woman was already straining her neck to see who else might be in the apartment.

Mr. Birger opened the door and Mrs. Stakavitzkaya stepped into the foyer. She saw Klara and Marina sitting at the kitchen table. "I hope I'm not disturbing your dinner," she called out to them.

Mrs. Birger walked toward the woman and tried to appear gracious. "Oh, no, Mrs. Stakavitzkaya. I'm afraid we're getting a late start tonight. Marina has only been home a few minutes."

"Well, that's one of the reasons I thought I should visit."

Marina, who was still at the kitchen table, sat up in

her chair. She could not imagine what interest this woman had in her.

"Please," Mr. Birger said gesturing to the sofas, "let's all make ourselves comfortable." Mrs. Stakavitzkaya sat on the larger sofa, and Mrs. Birger took the other one. Mr. Birger remained standing, and Marina stood by his side.

The woman began by clapping her hands and exclaiming in her boisterous manner, "I understand your lovely Marina has been chosen as the school representative in the storytelling contest. My granddaughter was a finalist six years ago. It's quite an honor." The woman sat there beaming as if she were Marina's proud great-aunt.

"We're all very pleased," replied Mr. Birger. He winked at Marina.

"As you should be! But I'm afraid your wife and you are being rather negligent." She was no longer smiling.

"I beg your pardon?" said Mrs. Birger.

"Well, it's not my place to interfere, Mrs. Birger, but after all, we are judged by the company we keep." Mrs. Stakavitzkaya purposely paused, hoping the Birgers would understand that she was referring to the Pasternack family. But no one commented. After a few awkward seconds, the woman added, "You must know what I mean. After the ordeal with that old man, everyone is talking." She waited again. The blank expressions on the family's faces infuriated the snoop. "Well,

I don't understand. Every tenant in the building has been questioned. I can't imagine no one spoke to you."

"They were here, as well," replied Klara.

"Then you understand my concern for Marina. She shouldn't be seen talking to that Pasternack boy. I certainly wouldn't allow it if she were my daughter." Mrs. Stakavitzkaya stood up in a huff and wagged her finger at Marina. "You know, of course, if you've heard or seen anything improper in that apartment, you must report it. It's your duty as a loyal Soviet."

Once more, Mrs. Stakavitzkaya waited for a response. After another long silence, she started for the foyer. "I'm sorry to have disturbed you," she said in a disgusted tone. "It's just that I saw Marina with that Pasternack boy again, and it was on my mind. By the way, how is the old man?"

"We really don't know, Mrs. Stakavitzkaya," Mr. Birger answered coldly. "Perhaps, if you're so concerned, you'll visit him at the hospital."

Mrs. Stakavitzkaya began to cackle. "No, thank you." On her way out, she noticed all the dishes on the kitchen table. "What pretty china," she remarked. "Are you preparing for a party, Mrs. Birger?"

"Oh, no," Klara answered nervously. She immediately walked back into the kitchen. "I was just dusting cupboards."

"Yes, I clean out my cabinets every so often as well. Isn't it incredible what you find? I put things away and

totally forget about them. Lucky for me I don't need
to hide anything." Mrs. Stakavitzkaya started cackling
again and walked out the door.

The hideous sound made Marina shiver. "What do
you think she wanted, Papa?"

"Sh. We'll talk later." He pointed to the door, in-
dicating that someone might be standing in the hallway. "Let's have dinner, Klara. It's late."

Mrs. Birger prepared the meal while Marina helped
her father put the dishes back into the cabinet. They
worked in silence, but they were all thinking about
Mrs. Stakavitzkaya. At dinner Marina asked her question again.

"Why do you think that horrible woman came
here?"

"I'm not exactly sure," Vasily admitted, "but it
seems to me she was trying to get information."

"Perhaps the KGB put her up to it," added Klara.

"No doubt," the husband answered. He reached
over and put his hand on Marina's shoulder. "You stay
away from her! And, remember, anything we say cannot be repeated."

"Papa, Misha would never betray us!"

"Marina!" her mother shrieked. "You are especially
not to talk to Misha. When he comes this evening, your
father or I will give him back the notebook."

"But, Mama," the daughter begged, "couldn't I at
least explain to him about the order from Mr. Anatassy?"

"Absolutely not!" yelled Mr. Birger. "Mr. Anatassy's name cannot be mentioned."

"But Misha will hate me!"

"Perhaps for a while," Mrs. Birger said. "When he learns the truth, he'll understand."

Marina pushed her dinner plate toward the center of the table and banged her fist. "I don't understand. First you take the storytelling contest away from me, and now you're telling me to give up my one true friend. Why are you punishing me?"

"Please, Marina," her father told her. "We're not punishing you. It's just that, once I present the invitation, our lives will be different."

Marina looked up at the cabinet of dishes. Suddenly she had a wonderful idea.

"Mama, when we get to Kansas City, can I contact your friend in Israel for Misha's family? Maybe they can leave too."

Both adults doubted that the Pasternacks would ever be granted exit visas. However, neither Vasily nor Klara expressed this fear to Marina.

"Of course, darling," Mrs. Birger agreed. "If that's what they want, we will try to help them, as much as possible."

Marina smiled. "Okay. I'll do whatever you want. After all," she reasoned, "if I act like I don't like him now, maybe I can help him get to Jerusalem. Then he'll understand I was really a good friend."

The Birgers were relieved to hear Marina talking

more positively about their plans, and during the remainder of their dinner Mrs. Birger spoke cheerfully about the family reuniting in America.

After the meal, Marina began her evening studies. First, she copied all the assignments from Misha's notepad. Then she opened her history book to begin Chapter Seven. The chapter was long and boring, and Marina had difficulty keeping her mind on her work. She started to worry about Misha coming to the apartment that night, and she wondered how she would handle the situation in school the next day.

All of a sudden Marina had the perfect solution. Tomorrow, if he asked her why she was ignoring him, she would tell him she had no time for him or Uncle Mordecai because of the storytelling contest. Certainly people like Stakavitzkaya and Anatassy would approve. Even Mr. Fyodorov would be pleased to hear that the contest meant more to her than friendship with Misha Pasternack.

But then Marina gasped. What about Mr. Fyodorov? Eventually he would have to know the truth, and then he would tell the whole school she was a liar and Jewish traitor. After all, she had assured him that her parents had no intentions of leaving the country. Marina broke into a cold sweat thinking how everyone would despise her.

She was so upset, she did not even hear the knocking, but both Mr. and Mrs. Birger went to the door. They suspected it was Misha, and Mrs. Birger told Marina to remain at the kitchen table.

"Hi! May I see Marina?" Misha was still trying to catch his breath. He had just run all the way from the hospital.

"I'm sorry. Marina is studying," replied Mr. Birger.

"But she has my assignment pad. I need it."

"Just a moment." Mrs. Birger went into the kitchen and picked up the pad. Marina never budged. Her back was to the front door, and she could not see Misha.

"Here you are," said Klara as she handed the boy his notepad. "Marina will see you at school."

Mr. Birger began to close the front door, but Misha put his hand out to stop it.

"I meant to tell you," he said cheerfully, "Uncle Mordecai is doing much better. You can visit anytime."

"We'll try our best," Mr. Birger mumbled. He hated being so rude, but Mrs. Stakavitzkaya's visit had frightened him.

Misha suddenly realized how peculiarly the Birgers were behaving. "Have I done something wrong?" he asked. "Is Marina angry with me?"

"Of course not!" replied Vasily. "But it's late. Go home, and do your homework." Mr. Birger slammed the door.

Marina shuddered at the noise. "Papa, you didn't have to be so nasty!"

"Your father had no choice," replied Mrs. Birger.

She could see that her husband was very upset. "Misha wouldn't leave. It was dangerous for us to be standing at the door and talking like that."

"Well, he could have come in for one minute."

Mr. Birger walked back into the kitchen and sat down next to his daughter. He held her pretty heart-shaped face in his hands and stared into her deep green eyes. "Misha is a very fine boy, and I wish his family well," he said calmly, "but we can no longer be friends with him or his family."

Meanwhile, a very perplexed boy walked downstairs.

"My goodness, that was a short visit," remarked his mother. She noticed her son was upset about something.

"They were very strange up there." Misha pointed to Marina's apartment and made a face.

"What do you mean? Are those men back?"

"I don't think so."

"Well, what is it, Misha? Stop scaring me."

"I don't know, Mother!" Misha shouted in an exasperated voice. "It's just that the Birgers wouldn't let me into their apartment, wouldn't let me see Marina, and even slammed the door in my face."

Mrs. Pasternack nodded as if she understood. "It's happening again," she muttered.

"What is?"

"You were too young. You don't remember. But after your father's death, no one wanted to know me or Uncle Mordecai. Even cousins ignored us. I got a lot of doors slammed in my face."

"Why?"

"The authorities. They scare everyone." Mrs. Pasternack paused and remembered how it felt when she had lost all her friends. "If they think you're too friendly with the wrong people," she explained, "you can end up in a labor camp. Don't blame the Birgers."

Misha refused to accept this excuse. "Friends are supposed to be brave for one another. If matters were reversed, I wouldn't desert Marina."

Mrs. Pasternack knew her son's heart was aching. In the last four months, she had watched his affections grow for the young upstairs neighbor. At times she had expressed her concern to Uncle Mordecai. She worried he was too young to feel so deeply. After all, schoolgirls choose new boyfriends every week.

The mother lovingly held her son close to her. She hugged and kissed him. "Don't be so glum," she said. "You're going to have lots and lots of girlfriends."

Misha frowned and pulled away from his mother. "I don't like the other girls, and I don't want lots and lots of girlfriends." He picked up his history book and turned to Chapter Seven.

7

OVIR

The alarm clock was buzzing. Marina forced her eyes to open and turned toward her parents' bed. Their sofa was already closed.

"Mama? Papa?" she called out groggily.

Mrs. Birger hurried in from the kitchen. "Oh, dear, we forgot to turn this off." She picked up the clock and pressed down on the alarm. "It's very early, Marina. Go back to sleep."

"What time is it?"

"Quarter to five."

Marina pulled the covers up to her neck and turned

over on her side. "Why's everyone up?" she yawned and closed her eyes again.

"Because the line will be very long, and your father doesn't want to wait for hours just to be sent away. We want the application today."

At the mention of the word "application," Marina's eyes opened wide. "But, Mama, no one will be there until nine A.M."

"And I want to be the first to receive the form," announced Mr. Birger as he stepped out of the bathroom. He walked over to Marina and kissed her on the forehead. "You'll be exhausted by this afternoon, honey. Go back to sleep."

But Marina couldn't fall back to sleep. She sat up in her bed and watched her father straighten his tie. She wondered what he was thinking.

Mrs. Birger had gone back into the kitchen to prepare breakfast, and Marina motioned for her father to sit beside her. "Papa," she whispered, "maybe we should wait a little longer."

Mr. Birger shook his head. "We made our decision. The time is now."

"Aren't you scared?"

"Am I scared?" he repeated slowly. "Of course. But I'm scared every day of my life. I worry about losing my job because someone decides there are too many Jews on the hospital staff. I worry that men watch me and follow me and one day will falsely accuse me because I am a Jew. I worry that I'll be a victim like Uncle

Mordecai—or, even worse, like Misha's father. Most of all, I fear that one day you will have to worry as I do."

Marina hugged her father and cried, "I'm already worried."

"No," Mr. Birger said firmly. "Today, at last, we must be hopeful."

At five o'clock, Mr. Birger kissed Klara and Marina good-by. He walked out of his apartment and automatically slammed the front door. The building was very still, and the noise from the door sounded like a gunshot. Mr. Birger moved very quietly down the stairs, hoping he had not disturbed any tenants.

"Vasily," someone whispered. He stopped and saw Ina Pasternack standing in the doorway. She motioned for him to come closer.

"You frightened me," Vasily said softly.

"I'm sorry. Usually the building is very quiet this time of morning."

"Are you always up this early?"

Ina nodded. "I'm a very early riser. When I taught at the University, I would correct my students' papers. It was a useful way to pass the time."

"A professor? But I thought you were a sales clerk."

Mrs. Pasternack sighed. "After my husband's death, I lost my position."

Mr. Birger nodded that he understood. Having heard Misha's story, it came as no surprise that the wife had been fired from a prestigious institute.

Nervously, he checked his watch. "We'd better not speak. We'll wake the others."

"One moment," Ina begged. "Misha told me about last night. He doesn't understand, but I want you to know ———" Suddenly she shut the door.

"Good morning, Comrade."

Mr. Birger quickly turned and saw Mrs. Stakavitzkaya at her door across the hall.

"I see Marina is not the only one who visits down here."

"Good morning, Madam." Mr. Birger ignored her cackling and continued down the steps.

The early-morning air felt cold and damp. The sky was still dark, and, except for the noise from a few passing cars, the streets were very quiet. Vasily walked briskly and thought about Ina Pasternack. The young widow had suffered so much in her short lifetime. In comparison, his life seemed blessed. Was he crazy to jeopardize whatever happiness he now enjoyed?

He pulled up his coat collar and quickened his pace. To avoid thinking about the cold, Vasily remembered a game he and Marina often played together. One person would name a location, such as a theater or a park or even a particular street corner, and the other would have to describe a happy memory associated with that location. Vasily always laughed, because Marina would always begin the game with the same two landmarks. First, she would name the Federal Academic Theater of Opera and Ballet, and Vasily would automatically recall the first time Marina stepped inside this spectacular theater with its plush red carpet and massive gold ornaments. Marina had been so awe-struck that Vasily had to bend down and tell his little daughter to close her mouth. Later that night, she was only worried she had accidentally swallowed a bug.

Marina loved that story, but she loved another even better. For her second choice of landmarks she always named the Potemkinskaya, the giant stairway at Odessa's seaport. On these steps, Vasily asked Klara to be his wife.

"Your mother looked wonderful," he would begin, "but she was complaining that the sea breeze made her long, dark hair look wild, like a witch. Her hair was as long as yours then," he always added. "Anyway, I assured her that she looked beautiful—as beautiful as any fairy princess. She blushed and asked me whether a prince would rescue her one day. To which I boldly replied, 'Not only shall I rescue you, but I shall marry you and we will live happily ever after.' "

Remembering these words made Vasily stop abruptly. "Happily ever after," he repeated to himself. Suddenly he had no doubts about the exit visa. If he planned to keep his promise, they had to take the gamble. Vasily continued walking at an even quicker pace.

At twenty-three minutes past five, Mr. Birger stood outside the front door of the police station. He paused to check inside his coat pocket for the invitation.

"Something wrong? Can I help you, Comrade?" A police officer approached and grasped the door handle.

"No. N-n-nothing's wrong," Vasily stuttered.

The policeman studied him for a second. "Why are you standing here?"

"I've come to wait at OVIR."

The policeman grunted and walked into the building, letting the door slam in Mr. Birger's face. Immediately, Vasily grasped the handle and walked to the back of the building.

He did not need directions to the office. Six months earlier, he and Mr. Anatassy had come to this building to fill out forms about a theft in medical supplies. When they had passed the OVIR office and seen the long line of applicants, Mr. Anatassy had shaken his head in disgust. At the time, Mr. Birger pretended not to notice Anatassy's reaction.

As he turned the corner, he saw a line of people outside the office. Vasily took his place behind a very pretty woman. She looked young; Vasily guessed she was nineteen at most.

Minutes later, two policemen approached. Mr. Birger recognized one as the man at the front door and immediately lowered his head.

"They're coming earlier and earlier," cried out the one who had spoken to Vasily. "Some of them even sleep here the night before they want to be seen."

"Good! They're all enemies of the State. Let's get rid of them one way or another," sneered the companion.

Suddenly, he spotted the young woman. "Hey, watch me have some fun." He called out, "Oh, Missy! Missy! What's a pretty thing like you doing here? How about coming with me for a sip of vodka?"

The two men roared with laughter, but the woman showed no reaction. She kept her head bowed and eyes lowered.

The officer insisted upon getting the young lady's attention.

"Hey, Missy, I'm talking to you."

The woman continued to look at the floor.

"Just who do you think you are? You can't ignore a policeman." He was about to grab the woman when a voice called out.

"Officers! Is there a problem here?"

The two men stood at attention.

"No, sir!" both shouted to their commanding officer.

"Gentlemen, we have nothing to do with OVIR. Get on with your duties!"

In seconds the two were at the other end of the hall.

When they were out of sight, Mr. Birger whispered to the woman, "You were very lucky." Still she made no response.

At nine o'clock, the OVIR office opened. By that time, the line stretched to the end of the long corridor. Yet, except for an occasional cough or sneeze, the hall was quiet.

Vasily was finally ushered into the office and told to be seated. He watched the young woman who had been in front of him present her invitation. The clerk in charge looked at it and began badgering her with questions.

"Please," the young woman said, "speak slower. I have to read lips."

Vasily then understood. The woman was deaf. He wondered if she even knew that two policemen had harassed her in the hallway.

"Next, please," shouted a clerk from across the room. Vasily quickly walked over to the desk.

"My name is Vasily Birger. I am here to request an application for the exit visa to Israel."

"Your invitation?"

Vasily handed him the paper and expected to be questioned like the deaf woman, but the clerk immediately handed him the lengthy form.

"You understand," the man said in an arrogant tone, "that if there is one mistake, our office will not accept your application."

"You mean I must do it over."

"No!" screamed the clerk. "I mean you will never get another one. In addition, when you return this form, bring a work reference from your employer. And your wife's employer, of course."

Mr. Birger picked up the eight-page application. He scanned it quickly to make sure he understood all the questions. "What do you mean the exact day and place of my grandmother's death? The woman died fifteen years before I was born."

The clerk sneered. "We check everything."

Mr. Birger put the application in his inside coat pocket and left. The deaf woman was still being questioned; outside, the line of waiting people wrapped around the far corner of the hallway.

At the conservatory that morning, Marina was having a very good piano lesson.

"Excellent!" the teacher applauded.

"Thank you, Mr. Kozigan."

"Don't stop practicing now that you're a celebrity."

Marina blushed. "What do you mean?"

"The contest! The other students have told me all about your victory. They're positive you'll take first prize."

Quickly Marina collected her books from the top of the piano. It seemed pointless to talk about the finals when she knew she would not be a participant. "I better hurry. Mrs. Horrowitz is waiting for me upstairs."

"No, she's not," the instructor replied.

"Is she ill?"

"No. I'm afraid she was discharged from her duties."

Marina gasped. "But she's a wonderful musician, and all the students love her."

"Obviously the feeling was not mutual. She requested her work reference." Marina assumed this meant that the woman planned to live in another city.

When she mentioned this to Mr. Kozigan, the teacher laughed.

"I'm surprised at you, Marina. You should know that people can't just relocate. There are housing quotas. Unless someone is willing to trade apartments, it is very unlikely that anyone can move."

"Well, why would she ask for a work reference?"

The teacher looked very surprised. "Come on, child. Your parents must have explained these matters to you. Those who wish exit visas must submit references from their employers."

"Oh," Marina muttered. She suddenly remembered that Mrs. Horrowitz was Jewish.

"Well, at last you understand!" Mr. Kozigan exclaimed. "The woman is a traitor and an enemy of the State. We should all feel relieved the school is rid of her."

As Marina walked upstairs to a practice room, she wondered how long it would be until Mr. Kozigan would repeat the same thing about her. More important, she worried about her own parents losing their jobs. How would they survive if visas were not granted?

Marina sat at the concert grand and opened her music book. She set the metronome at a rapid speed and began to practice. She had played these exercises so often, she did not need to read the music. Her fingers automatically played the intricate patterns.

For almost ten minutes, she played without a single mistake. Then she hit a wrong note. Two beats later, she hit another, and then another. With both hands, Marina banged the keyboard.

"I know how you feel," said a slender young man standing behind her.

"How long have you been here?" asked Marina. She had not seen anyone enter the room.

"I heard most of it. It was quite good."

"Until I messed up."

"That's what happens, I'm afraid. One wrong move can ruin everything." The remark made Marina think of the exit visa.

"Who are you?" she asked nervously.

"I'm Ivan Chernetzky."

"A new student?" Marina knew he looked older than the other pupils, but he seemed too informal to be a teacher.

"Yes and no," he laughed. "I'm still a student myself, but I've been asked to assist until a suitable teacher can be found. I was told to meet a Marina Birger for a tutorial at eleven, but she never appeared."

Marina blushed. "You were waiting for me. Mr. Kozigan didn't tell me there would be a substitute. I came here instead."

The young man chuckled. "At least you put your time to good use. We can begin tomorrow. Play some more."

But the moment the young man left the practice hall,

Marina decided to pack her tote bag. If she hurried, she could spend time with her father before school. Marina automatically assumed he had not reported to work for the day and was at home completing the application. She was anxious to see that he had returned safely from OVIR.

Two blocks from her building Marina heard someone shout her name.

"Marina! Over here!"

Marina looked across the street and saw a long line of people standing outside a shoe store. Then she saw Shura waving frantically and crossed the street.

"Hi! They just got a shipment of wonderful sheepskin boots. I hope they don't sell out before it's my turn." Shura kept shifting from one foot to another in an effort to stay warm.

Marina surveyed the line. "Are you kidding? You've got at least a two-hour wait. You'll be late for school."

"No, I won't! My mom works close by. She'll take over at her lunch break. Until then, do you want to keep me company?"

"Hey!" screamed a teen-aged boy standing in back of Shura. "Your friend can't cut into line."

"Don't worry," Marina assured the boy, "I'm not staying." Marina turned to leave, but Shura started whining.

"Oh, Marina. Just a few minutes. It's so boring waiting by myself."

"Only one minute," Marina agreed good-naturedly.

Suddenly Shura turned to the boy behind her. "You should have more respect," she yelled and then pointed to Marina. "This girl is a finalist in Odessa's storytelling contest, and she's going to win."

Marina blushed. "Shura, stop it!"

The boy ignored Marina's embarrassment. "Really?" he asked her. "I was a semifinalist at my school three years ago. Which school will you represent?"

"The best, of course—the Odessa Middle School Number Twenty-three!" Shura made this announcement as loud as she could.

"They never win!" someone yelled.

"This year we will," Shura insisted. "This year we've got the best storyteller in all of Odessa." She went to grab Marina's hand, but Marina had quietly stepped out of line and was already across the street.

"Come back," Shura screamed.

"Sorry, got to go," Marina yelled and turned the corner.

As she opened the door to her apartment house, Marina was greeted by Mrs. Stakavitzkaya, who, as usual, was sitting and knitting in a corner of the lobby.

"Good day, Marina."

Marina nodded. "How are you, Mrs. Stakavitzkaya?" she asked and started up the steps. Her tone was respectful, but not very friendly.

"Tired. I woke up much too early. I guess your father had the same trouble."

Marina stopped on the stairway. "What do you mean?"

"I saw him this morning. He and that Pasternack woman should have more sense than to be socializing in the hall at such an hour. They probably disturbed the entire floor. I know they disturbed me."

Marina did not answer the woman, but raced up the stairs to the fifth floor.

"Papa, Papa," she called out as she unlocked the apartment door. Alone in her living room, Marina imagined that the vicious woman had made up some terrible story and her father was being held by the KGB at that very moment. Not knowing what else to do, Marina ran to the hospital to alert her mother.

"Marina! What's wrong? Why are you at the hospital?"

Marina stopped and turned her head. Walking toward her was Mr. Birger, accompanied by Mr. Anatassy.

"Papa!" she cried as she ran to him with open arms. "I'm so glad to see you."

"Are you feeling all right, young lady?" asked Mr. Anatassy. "You look very flushed."

"That's just from running, sir." Suddenly Marina realized she could not explain herself in front of Mr. Anatassy.

"Why are you here?" her father asked again.

Marina did not know what to do, and began to giggle. "Just wanted to say hello before school, Papa. I'll go see Mama for a minute." Before she could be questioned further, Marina raced toward the pharmacy lab.

But she never visited her mother, because standing outside the lab were Misha and Ina Pasternack, talking to Uncle Mordecai's physician. Immediately Marina walked in the opposite direction. She hoped Misha had not seen her.

On her way back to school, Marina remembered she had not eaten any lunch and stopped at a vendor's cart.

"I'll have a glass of seltzer and a package of nuts, please."

"That's not a very healthy lunch," a voice said. Marina thought it was her history teacher, Mrs. Krezshnovskaya, and turned to say hello.

"You sneak, Misha! You tricked me again. Why didn't you say hello in a normal voice?"

"Why didn't you say hello at the hospital?"

Marina stuttered. "Th-th-that was different. You and your mother were speaking to the doctor."

"Sure, and what about last night?"

Marina paid the vendor and started walking. Misha ran after her. The sidewalks were crowded, and it was difficult for Misha to stay by Marina's side.

"Come on, Marina. Stop and talk to me for a minute. If I did something wrong, you can at least tell me. I thought we were friends."

Marina wanted to explain everything. She wanted

him to know that Mr. Anatassy had ordered her family not to visit Uncle Mordecai, that Mrs. Stakavitzkaya was probably spying on her family for the KGB, and that today her father had applied for the exit visa. But Marina did not stop.

Finally, on the school steps, Misha grabbed Marina's arm. "You're being a coward!" he yelled.

At that moment, Mr. Fyodorov and Mrs. Krezshnovskaya were coming up the steps. As loud as she could, Marina shouted, "For the last time, leave me alone. I won't have any time for you or your uncle. My only concern is to prepare for the storytelling contest! I thought my father made that perfectly clear last night." Marina saw the principal and teacher exchange smiles.

At first Misha did not respond. Then, just as Marina stepped up to the front door, he screamed to her, "Don't worry about it, little 'Miss Crybaby,' I'll never bother you again. In fact, I don't plan to ever talk to you again."

Marina pretended not to hear the comments, but after changing her shoes she rushed to the girls' rest room, locked herself inside a stall, and burst into tears.

"Hey, what's wrong in there?" a girl asked.

"Nothing," Marina answered in a weepy voice. "I just have a stomach ache."

"Go see the nurse."

Just then the warning bell rang.

Purposely, Marina stayed in the stall a few more

moments. Then slowly she unlocked the door and found herself alone in the bathroom. At the sink, she splattered cold water on her eyes and cheeks. The icy drops trickled down her neck and gave her the shivers.

While patting her neck dry, she touched the delicate chain to her locket. Marina then grasped the necklace and remembered how she had boasted that the charm would be her "heart of courage." She walked out of the bathroom, clutching the golden heart.

The second bell rang just as Marina entered the science lab.

"You're late, Marina!" Mr. Shatz looked very annoyed.

"But, Mr. Shatz ———"

"No buts, young lady. Go to the office."

Marina obediently turned to leave the room.

"And please," ordered the teacher, "make sure that Mr. Fyodorov is aware of this misconduct. I expect a note from him personally."

The other students stared at their teacher in amazement. Mr. Shatz was one of the kindest teachers at school and never sent anyone to the principal's office. No one understood why today he would single out Marina for punishment. But Marina knew exactly why this man was making an example of her. He still wanted the principal to choose another student for the storytelling contest.

Marina walked up to the school secretary and asked for Mr. Fyodorov.

"I'm sorry, dear," Miss Seordnaya said pleasantly. "Mr. Fyodorov asked not to be disturbed."

"But Mr. Shatz expects a signed note!"

"Then you'll have to wait." The secretary continued her work and Marina sat down next to a tall filing cabinet at the other end of the room.

She did not wait long. Just two minutes later, Mr. Fyodorov appeared at his door, shaking a man's hand. When Marina saw the visitor she immediately crouched behind the filing cabinet.

"I'll see what I can do," the man said to Fyodorov. "I'm not making promises. Besides, they have to return the form before I can take any action."

Marina watched the principal and visitor leave the outer office.

Suddenly, Miss Seordnaya stood up and saw Marina hiding behind the cabinet. "What are you doing?" she laughed.

Marina shrugged. Her face was bright red.

"Okay, okay," the secretary chuckled. "I'll give you a note for Mr. Shatz, and I'll explain that Mr. Fyodorov was unable to see you. But no more nonsense, or we'll both be in trouble."

"It was terrible! I looked up and saw that man in Mr. Fyodorov's office."

"What man?" asked Mr. Birger. He put down his newspaper and started to pay attention to Marina's story. She had been babbling about being tardy for science class.

"The man who searched our house. The same one I saw talk to Mrs. Stakavitzkaya. He was at school today."

"So?" said Klara. "That night he mentioned he knew the principal. It was probably a social call."

"He may have been there checking on us, Mama."

"Marina!" scolded her father. "You must stop thinking everyone is spying on us."

"Well, Mrs. Stakavitzkaya is! When you weren't home, I was sure she had called the KGB. That's why I came to the hospital."

"Whatever made you think your father wouldn't report to work?"

"I assumed ———"

"That's the problem," said Mr. Birger sternly. "You assume too much, and your imagination gets the better of you."

Marina pouted for a minute and then changed the subject. "Did you get the form?"

"Yes," Vasily answered softly. "But it's worthless."

"Why?" demanded Klara. Mr. Birger had not yet told his wife that he did not have the information required. When he explained the problem, she giggled.

"Why are you laughing at me?"

"I'm sorry, darling," she said. "It's just that I've been keeping a secret from you." Mrs. Birger unlocked the china cabinet and put her hand in the old silver teapot.

She pulled out a tiny notebook. "In here you will find all the information you need."

Mr. Birger opened the pad and saw family names, dates, and places of births and deaths. "But how did you know?"

"I helped Lena do their form. I knew one day we would need the information for your side of the family as well. Among other things, your wife is a good detective." The Birgers hugged and kissed and laughed and then hugged some more. Only Marina looked unhappy.

"Don't fret, darling!" Klara said. "Before you know it, you'll be seeing your Cousin Joseph. I'm sure he'll introduce you to all his new friends."

"But what about Misha? He called me a coward and screamed he would never talk to me again."

"Only for now," Mrs. Birger comforted her daughter. "When he learns the truth, he'll realize how courageous you really are. He'll admire you."

Mr. and Mrs. Birger did not want to burden Marina any more than necessary. They waited until she had fallen asleep to fill out the application. Even with all the information in Klara's secret notebook, it still took them four hours to complete the form. They finished at two o'clock in the morning.

"We've been up almost an entire night, and I'm tired," Klara yawned. "But I feel good, very good."

Vasily stared at the application. "Don't relax yet," he cautioned. "This was the easy part."

8
Every Monday

Mr. Anatassy gasped. "Are you sure?"

Mr. Birger nodded.

"All right, then," he barked. "I'll have the information completed in one week." The supervisor did not bother to look up as he motioned for Mr. Birger to leave his office.

In all their years together, Vasily had never known his boss to be late for a deadline. If Anatassy said a week, he meant a week. But Klara was worried.

"I remember Aleksandr had a lot of trouble securing

his work reference. He finally threatened to go to the district prosecutor."

"Klara, be patient and give the man his time." For his wife's sake, Mr. Birger acted optimistic, but he, too, was concerned. By law, a work supervisor was required to provide the information, but everyone knew that managers often procrastinated for as long as possible. Usually the authorities blamed these men and women for not being more aware of subordinates' attitudes; ultimately, their records suffered. Mr. Birger regretted the unfairness of the situation, but he knew no way to avoid it.

The next five days passed slowly for the Birgers. Marina secretly hoped that Mr. Anatassy would find an excuse not to complete the forms by the end of the week. She figured that the longer he took to complete the references, the more time she had before confronting Mr. Fyodorov. She hoped the principal might still reconsider his selection of a Jewish finalist and disqualify her—just as her cousin had been disqualified from the semifinals years ago. That way she would never have to reveal her parents had applied for an exit visa. When she mentioned this possibility to her father, he became very excited.

"What do you mean tell him? You're not to tell anyone!"

"But, Papa, I thought you agreed that if I perform in the finals, we might never get a visa."

"Of course!" snapped Mr. Birger. "But it is four months before the finals. If nothing has changed, you can drop out of the contest at the end of the school year. And still you won't tell Fyodorov the real reason. We must keep our plans a secret."

Her father sounded so upset, Marina did not dare continue the conversation. Still, she dreaded the day she would have to face Mr. Fyodorov. She knew it was unlikely her family would receive their visas before June. Most Jews were fortunate if they left after six or seven months. Her only hope was to be disqualified.

The afternoon before the references were due, Vasily stopped at Anatassy's office to discuss a new purchase for the hospital.

"I'm sorry, Mr. Birger," said the receptionist at the front desk. "Mr. Anatassy just left."

"I'll see him tomorrow. Thank you."

"Oh, no," she replied. "He won't be back until the end of next week."

"But he's supposed to have something prepared for me tomorrow!"

The receptionist shrugged. "I know nothing about it."

Vasily stormed toward the lab to find Klara, but as he grew closer to the pharmacy, he calmed himself and turned toward his own office. He knew it was useless to upset his wife at work.

Once inside his tiny office, he shut the door, sat down at his desk, and began to rub the sides of his head.

In the last six days he had begun to suffer from throbbing headaches. He told Klara they were due to fatigue, but he knew better. The strain of their ordeal was already having its effect on him.

He heard a knock at his door and opened his eyes. "Come in." Standing in the doorway was Mr. Anatassy. In his right hand he was waving a Manila envelope.

"I've already seen Klara. Here is your work reference."

"But they told me you had gone."

"And I told you one week. You should know I'm never late. Just make sure you and your wife are out of here by the end of the day. This hospital doesn't look kindly on traitors." Mr. Anatassy threw the envelope on the desk and left.

Vasily had expected to be discharged, but not in such an abrupt manner. After all, he and Mr. Anatassy had shared a close working relationship for many years. He closed the door again and ripped open the envelope. As he read the work reference, his headache worsened.

The report said that in the last month Vasily's performance had deteriorated, and that it was just a matter of time before he would have received his dismissal. The supervisor called him lazy and sloppy and suggested that his declining work habits were a direct result of a developing drinking problem.

Vasily was still staring at Anatassy's signature when he heard Klara's voice at the door.

"Come in," he mumbled.

Klara walked in and closed the door. She was holding her tote bag and dressed to leave the hospital. "Are you ready, Vasily?"

He looked up at her and held out his reference. "What did yours say?"

"It was bad. Just like yours, I'm sure."

"He called me a drunk."

Klara shook her head in disgust. "I remember they complained that Aleksandr was too sickly and Lena flirted with all the male musicians. Can you imagine they said she distracted the men at rehearsals?"

"But, Klara, this is Anatassy. I trusted him. How could he write these lies?"

"Don't be ridiculous!" snapped Mrs. Birger. "We plan to leave, but Anatassy must stay. If he were to write the truth, they would punish him. Now, collect your things and be happy. He fulfilled his obligation."

Vasily quickly packed up his belongings and put on his coat and gloves. He glanced at his empty desk top and suddenly realized he would never return to this small, familiar room.

Klara had been studying her husband's expression. "Don't have any doubts, darling," she said softly. "You once told me never to look back."

Mr. Birger smiled. "We'll have to begin all over again."

Mrs. Birger nodded and started toward the door. "Let's go," she whispered. They walked out of the hospital, each clutching the other's hand. Neither looked back.

As they walked into their building, Mrs. Stakavitzkaya rushed up to them. "Old Man Pasternack came home this morning. It's incredible. When they took him out of here, I thought for sure he would never return."

"The human body has a will of its own," said Mr. Birger, trying to ignore the woman's callousness.

"Well, of course, Comrade, but in this circumstance, I didn't think the authorities would be so lax. Old or not, the man committed a crime against the State. He should be in a work camp."

"We wouldn't know anything about that," Mrs. Birger replied in an annoyed tone.

"Well, I do!" shouted Mrs. Stakavitzkaya, and she grasped her bulging hips. Her right foot started tapping the linoleum floor.

Mr. Birger smiled sweetly at her. "Don't get so excited," he said soothingly. "It's foolish to get yourself sick over other people's problems." He then bowed slightly and added, "Try to have a good day."

The gossip grunted. She did not budge from her pose as Vasily took his wife's arm and led her up the steps.

Mrs. Birger tried to maintain her serious expression. Out of the corner of her eye, however, she noticed Vasily was also trying not to grin. Suddenly they both lost control, and squeals of laughter echoed through the lobby. The more they tried to regain their composure, the louder their laughter became.

Mrs. Stakavitzkaya ignored them. Still standing with her hands on her hips she muttered under her breath, "They think they're so clever, but I'll fix them yet." Then she realized something was not right and called up to them.

"Comrades, isn't it too early for you to be home?"

The question startled Klara, and her laughter ceased. But Vasily replied with a chuckle, "Our schedule has changed somewhat."

"Oh? Is that why you left before dawn last week?"

"Yes. Exactly."

Mrs. Stakavitzkaya raised her hand, ready to wag her finger at Mr. Birger and reprimand him for being so noisy at 5:00 A.M. But just then she was distracted by two other tenants entering the building. She ran over to them and started complaining about Uncle Mordecai's return. Meanwhile, the Birgers hurried up to their apartment.

"We shouldn't have behaved like that," said Mrs. Birger as she hung up the coats. Suddenly Vasily put his hands on his hips and started tapping his foot. The pose made Klara burst into a new fit of laughter. Just as she regained her composure, Vasily took the pose once more and began wagging his finger in the air. This time Klara laughed even harder. Finally Mrs. Birger got a tissue from her tote bag and wiped the tears from her eyes.

"Please, Vasily, we must be serious. We have so much ahead of us."

"That is all the more reason we need to laugh," replied Mr. Birger. He took the pose again, but this time Klara frowned.

"Ooh, that disgusting woman! How dare she question you!"

Vasily heaved a long sigh. "Get used to it, Klara. She won't be the only one." He walked into the kitchen and sat down at the table. His wife noticed he was rubbing the sides of his head.

"It hurts again?"

"Don't worry. Just fatigue," mumbled Vasily, and he closed his eyes.

An hour later, Marina collapsed onto the sofa. Her arms were piled with books.

"I take it you have a lot of homework," her mother commented.

"Three tests," she yawned.

"We'll eat quickly so you can get right to work."

"Thank you," and Marina yawned again. "Any word about the references?"

"Why, yes!" said Mrs. Birger. She was just about to tell Marina that they planned to submit the papers when Mr. Birger spoke. "I'm afraid Mr. Anatassy will be away for a while."

"What will you do?"

Mr. Birger shrugged. "Nothing we can do but wait."

Marina turned to her mother. "I'm sorry, Mama. I know you're anxious for it all to happen quickly." She tried to sound convincing, but Mr. Birger could see his daughter looked relieved.

It was not until Marina had fallen asleep that Klara asked, "Vasily, why did you lie?"

"Our decision is still difficult for Marina. Why should she worry? When we have the visas we'll tell her. There's no reason for her to know that we're not at the hospital. She's at school all day."

"You're very foolish, Vasily. How long do you think you can carry on such a charade?"

"What does it matter?" replied Mr. Birger. "Each day is one day less for her to think about it."

The next morning Mr. and Mrs. Birger waved good-by to their daughter and started walking toward the hospital. Marina did not suspect that her parents were about to submit the application at the district OVIR office.

Klara and Vasily stood in line for hours. It was past noon when the Birgers finally presented their papers to the clerk. He did not remember Vasily, but looked at the stamped date on the application.

"Back so quickly?" he scoffed. "It usually takes applicants longer. I hope you haven't made any mistakes." The clerk grabbed the form and tossed it into a messy pile of papers. Vasily recognized the man from his first visit and remained silent, but Klara had a question for the clerk.

"Please, sir, what happens now?"

"What happens, Madam, is that you wait and wait and wait and wait. You could wait a lifetime!"

"What my wife means is, how do we find out if we've received the exit visas?"

"Not from this office! Next, please!"

Mr. Birger took his wife's arm and started toward the door. He did not want to create a scene in the office. Fortunately, another clerk had overheard the question.

"You people, come here." He pointed at Vasily and Klara. They immediately went over to the man's desk. "Don't return here," he said. "Every Monday morning at the City OVIR, in the downtown office, an official will read the list of names."

"What time?" asked Mrs. Birger.

"Nine A.M. You'll be smart to be there at least an hour early. There's a lot of people."

"Thank you." Mr. Birger put out his hand, but the man ignored it. "Just doing my job properly," he said loudly enough so that the first clerk could hear him.

The Birgers hurried down the long corridor toward the main entrance. A tall man was walking in the opposite direction. Vasily did not pay much attention to him, but Klara thought the man's face looked familiar. As he grew closer, his eyes met hers. Immediately she looked down at the floor.

Outside she whispered, "Did you see him?"

"Who?"

"That tall man who just passed us in the hallway."

Vasily shook his head.

"Well, he's the one who searched our house."

Mr. Birger started to rub the sides of his head. "Come on, Klara. I've had enough of this place."

They were just a block from their apartment when Klara said, "I hope Mrs. Stakavitzkaya is not in the lobby. I dread seeing her."

"Then let's stay out! How about lunch at Krasnaya?"

"The money," moaned Mrs. Birger. "We must be careful."

"Come on," coaxed Vasily. "It won't cost that much. We haven't eaten out in so long."

Klara could not resist the invitation. Krasnaya was her favorite restaurant, and it was true that she had not dined there in months. Ever since Lena's first letter from the United States, Klara had planned their finances very carefully. She knew from her sister's experience that they would have to save as much money as possible before submitting the application.

Klara had always been frugal, but in the last four months she had denied herself the smallest luxury. Even last December, when the neighborhood was cramming into the Moscow, the local movie house, to see *The Sound of Music,* Klara chose to stay home. Everyone was raving about the Western film's magnificent color, and Vasily planned the outing as a special treat for both Klara and Marina. At the last moment, Klara complained about a headache and insisted that

Marina and Vasily go without her. Of course, Mr. Birger had suspected the truth. His wife preferred to save the cost of admission. This afternoon he was pleased she had finally agreed to a small splurge.

On the trolley, the husband and wife did not speak but stared out the windows. Everything about the ride was so familiar, and yet both adults studied the scenery as if viewing it for the first time. As they approached the downtown square, Vasily pointed to two men sitting on a bench.

"In a few months, they will have their boards ready," he remarked.

Klara smiled. She knew how Vasily loved to watch the chess games in the square. He often boasted that as a child he had learned his best strategies studying "the plays" in the square.

Klara also liked the town square, but for different reasons. Each spring she looked forward to its rows of colorful flowers and sculptured fountains. She liked watching the young couples strolling hand in hand, and the little toddlers who squealed with delight as they chased one another around the statues.

But it was still a wintry day, and except for the two men on the bench, everyone seemed to be hurrying to warmer surroundings. Vasily and Klara stepped off the trolley car and walked briskly to the restaurant.

As soon as they entered, Vasily knew it would be just a matter of minutes before Klara would mention the flowers at each table. Both she and Marina loved fresh flowers, and the bouquets at Krasnaya were always exquisite.

Of course, when Marina dined at Krasnaya, she was more interested in the dance floor. Like a lot of Odessa's restaurants, Krasnaya featured a live band in the evenings. At night, however, the bar did a thriving business, and children were not welcomed. Marina often protested. "It's not fair that children miss the best part," she would whine.

As they were guided across the dance floor, Vasily thought about his daughter, but Klara was already pointing to the tables. "Oh, Vasily, aren't the yellow roses lovely?"

Mr. Birger smiled, but instantly stopped grinning. Sitting in a nearby corner, with three other companions, was Mr. Anatassy. The man looked up and saw Vasily. Mr. Birger nodded politely, but Anatassy ignored the acknowledgment. As the maître d'hôtel pointed to the table for two, Vasily quietly asked, "Do you possibly have something on the other side of the restaurant?"

"But, darling, this is fine," insisted Klara. She still had not noticed Anatassy in the corner.

"I'm sorry, sir. The other tables are reserved for larger parties."

"Thank you. This will do." Mr. Birger sat down and lowered his head.

"Vasily, what's wrong?"

"Mr. Anatassy is sitting in that corner there."

Klara turned and saw the supervisor. "Of all the bad luck! Just pay no attention to him. We owe him nothing!"

They ordered their platters of lox and herring and bowls of borscht. After the waiter had left, Klara leaned forward to sniff the roses. Vasily grinned and sipped his glass of white wine.

"Don't talk to me about employment quotas!" they heard a familiar voice declare. "I used to think quotas were too rigid—especially for the more educated Jews, but I was wrong. These people don't deserve to be anything but street cleaners. They've all shown their true colors since this visa business!"

"Perhaps we should leave," Klara whispered. But at that moment, their food arrived.

"That was a terrible waste of money," Klara grumbled later as they walked to the trolley stop.

"I'm shocked," replied Vasily. "I always thought of him as such a fine man. In there he sounded like another Stakavitzkaya."

Mrs. Birger did not bother to answer him. She was too upset. They had squandered their money on an unenjoyable lunch.

The Birgers returned to their building, and Klara was relieved to see that no one was sitting in the lobby. Mr. Birger picked up the mail in their box and followed his wife upstairs. As they were approaching the fourth floor landing, they noticed Mrs. Pasternack outside her door. She was smoking a cigarette and waved to them. Mr. Birger called out, "Good day!"

"Did you know Uncle Mordecai is home?" she asked them.

"How is he?" responded Vasily. Mrs. Birger said nothing. She was amazed her husband had even stopped to speak to this woman.

"Feisty as ever. He insisted I do my smoking out of the apartment. He said he doesn't mind it for himself, but he doesn't want Misha inhaling the impure air."

"I agree."

Ina blushed and admitted, "I know it's an unhealthy habit, but it's the only thing that calms my nerves. Maybe one day I won't need it." She took one last puff and then crushed the cigarette into a small ashtray she had been holding in her other hand. "I'd better check on my uncle," she said quickly and went back into her apartment.

"I never knew she smoked," whispered Klara as they walked up the last flight.

"There's a lot we don't know about that family," Vasily muttered.

When they walked inside their apartment, Vasily remembered he had letters in his hand. One envelope caught his eye immediately. It had no formal address on it—only the names "Vasily and Klara Birger." Vasily opened it at once.

"I don't believe it!" he shouted.

"What is it?" asked Mrs. Birger.

"Look what I found in the mailbox." He handed her a small slip of paper and the envelope full of money. On the paper were three words: "You'll be missed." At the bottom was a scribbled "A."

"Anatassy?" asked Klara excitedly.

"It must be. No one else knows."

"But, Vasily, you heard him in the restaurant."

Mr. Birger shook his head. "I was wrong to doubt him. I always believed he was a fine man, but it's like you said yesterday. He must maintain appearances. If the authorities thought he was sympathetic, who knows what could happen to him?"

Klara counted the money and squealed, "This certainly is a generous gift—almost a month's earnings. What a nice man!"

"He's more than nice!" snapped Vasily. "It took courage to give us this. You know they check the mail."

"Of course, darling. I understand that. Please don't be angry with me."

Mr. Birger put his arms out to his wife. "I didn't mean to bark at you. It's just that I'm disgusted. Someone helps me out, and I can't even shake his hand. It's like we're suddenly stricken with a plague!"

At school, Marina had to contend with just the opposite problem. Since Mr. Fyodorov's announcement, everyone paid lots of attention to her. Shura's outburst outside the shoe store had been but one incident. Almost every day someone mentioned her fine story. Marina acted very shy when children praised her. Students mistook this uneasiness for modesty, and she became all the more appealing to them.

Only Misha ignored her. He had not spoken to Marina since their fight on the steps. The same afternoon Mr. and Mrs. Birger received the unexpected gift, Misha broke the silence.

"Hey, wait up!" he called out as he followed Marina across the street. Marina did not hear him and continued walking. Misha caught up with her inside the lobby.

"You could have waited," he barked.

Marina turned around to him. "Are you talking to me?" she asked in a startled voice. When Marina saw that no one else was in the lobby, she hoped this would be her opportunity to reconcile with Misha. "Did you want to talk about something?" she asked shyly.

"Not really," Misha replied, "but I promised Uncle Mordecai I would tell you he's home. He'd like you to visit him."

Marina inched closer to Misha and began to whisper, "Oh, I wish I could, but ——"

At that moment the front door opened and in walked Mrs. Stakavitzkaya. Marina stepped back. "How many times do I have to tell you?" she yelled at Misha. "Leave me alone."

Misha watched Marina run up the steps and then darted past her. She hoped he would understand that

Mrs. Stakavitzkaya's intrusion had forced her to be so rude. She hoped he would be waiting upstairs, but as Marina approached the fourth-floor landing, she saw his door slam shut.

That first Monday, Vasily and Klara doubted they would hear anything. It had only been days since they submitted their papers. But as the clerk recommended, Vasily was in line by 8:00 A.M. at the city OVIR. When Marina asked why her father was leaving alone and so early, Klara explained that his schedule had changed on Mondays.

Vasily took the trolley car downtown, and at ten minutes to eight walked up the steps to the old police station. At the front desk he asked directions to OVIR. The clerk pointed to a room at the end of the hall. As Vasily drew closer to the line of people, he saw a familiar face. He did not think she would recognize him, but when the deaf woman saw him, she smiled.

"Hello," she said softly.

"Hello," Vasily replied.

Except for that one greeting, Vasily talked to no one. But many of those waiting were friendly with one another. After months of "Monday mornings," these people shared a bond.

At 9:00 A.M., an officer appeared at the door, and there was a sudden hush. Those families granted visas were read first. People wept. Then the officer announced his second list, and again people wept. These citizens had been denied visas.

Vasily's name had been on neither list. He was outside the police station and saw the young woman standing at the trolley stop. As a friendly gesture, he walked over to her and tapped on her shoulder. Vasily assumed that she, too, had not been mentioned. He formed his words slowly, so that she would understand.

"I suppose we shall see each other next week again," he said.

The woman's eyes filled with tears. "No," she sobbed. "They rejected my application. I must petition to a higher OVIR. Only those people who have never been rejected come here. Next time I wait, it will be in a different office."

For a second, Vasily was too shocked to answer but then replied, "You'll have better luck."

"Perhaps." The woman turned away and wiped her eyes. Just then the trolley car stopped. Vasily stood on the corner and watched the woman board. He felt a tear falling down his cheek.

Klara anxiously waited for the beginning of each week, but Vasily dreaded that moment on Monday when the officer announced those denied visas. The last Monday in April, Vasily heard the officer call out Birger. His name had been read from the second list. He felt his whole body trembling as he spoke to the officer.

"Excuse me, sir. My name is Vasily Birger. You just listed me as a rejection. Could you please tell me where I get forms to petition the decision?"

The officer looked puzzled. "Vasily? Vasily?" he repeated. "I read no Vasily."

"But you said Birger."

The officer looked at his list. "Birger!" he exclaimed. "Yes here it is. Michale Birger."

Vasily let out a cry of relief. "It's another Birger. Thank you. I must have missed the first name."

"Next week pay closer attention!"

The following Monday, Vasily did not have to pay attention for very long. After only a few seconds, he heard it. Vasily, Klara, and Marina Birger had received permission to leave Odessa.

A secretary issued all the necessary forms. She warned Vasily that he had exactly thirty days to fulfill the requirements or the visa would be revoked. She reminded him that if any papers were out of order, the family would not be permitted to leave the country.

Vasily rushed home to Klara. They hugged and cried. Klara kept stating how lucky they were to have heard so quickly. She had estimated that their wait would be at least six months.

"Never argue with the authorities," teased Vasily, and they hugged and kissed some more.

Anxiously they waited for Marina to return from school. In the last eight weeks she had never guessed her parents' secret and still believed Mr. Anatassy had not completed the references.

That afternoon she walked into the apartment in a foul mood. She sat down at the kitchen table and pounded her fist. "Papa! Mama! The school year is almost over, and I can't wait any longer. All anyone talks about is the storytelling contest. I can't take it anymore. What am I supposed to do?"

Vasily winked at Klara, and the woman giggled.

"What's so funny?" cried Marina, who had been silently brooding about the storytelling contest for the last two weeks.

Mr. Birger sat down next to his daughter and spoke. "I think tomorrow you must go to your principal and tell him you will not be able to attend the contest, that you will be out of the city."

"I can't just tell him that! It's too lame an excuse. Anyway, he'll want to know where."

"To Israel, of course," replied Mrs. Birger.

"But Papa said I'm not supposed to mention the application."

"That was before."

"Before what?"

"Before we were issued the visas!" exclaimed Mr. Birger.

Marina sat with her mouth open. "But how? You said you still hadn't returned the papers."

"That wasn't true," admitted Vasily, "but we didn't want to worry you."

"Then it's over!" declared Marina excitedly. "I don't need to worry anymore."

The Birgers did not mention that the next thirty days could be the most difficult of all.

Suddenly Marina jumped up from her chair. "Misha!

I can finally tell him. And I'll tell him that we'll have someone in Israel mail his family an invitation."

Mrs. Birger glanced over at her husband. She was still worried that association with the Pasternacks might cause their visas to be revoked. Mr. Birger thought one visit would be all right, but he reminded his daughter to make no mention of Kansas City.

Marina ran downstairs to the Pasternacks. She was about to knock when Misha opened the door. He was on his way out to buy a newspaper for Uncle Mordecai.

"What do you want?" he demanded.

"I came to tell you something. May I come in?"

"Who's there, Misha?" called out Mrs. Pasternack. She walked to the opened door and saw Marina. "What a surprise! Come in, Marina."

"Mother, I'll be back soon," said Misha, purposely ignoring Marina.

"You wait, boy!" cried Uncle Mordecai from the living room. "Misha, escort our guest in here."

Looking angry, Misha led Marina into the living room. When she saw Uncle Mordecai sitting in a rocker, Marina started to cry.

"Why the tears?" asked the old man.

"It's just I'm so happy you're well again. You looked so terrible that night."

"I've been waiting months to thank you. Why haven't you visited me?"

"I couldn't," Marina answered.

"She's too busy being the star for Odessa's storytelling contest," sneered Misha. "If Fyodorov thought she associated with Jews who cared about their religion, she'd be disqualified."

"That's not true!" protested Marina. "I just couldn't let anyone suspect ———"

"Suspect what?" demanded Misha.

"That my parents applied for a visa. It's why I'm here." Marina was so excited she did not stop to breathe between phrases. "We're leaving in a month, and as soon as I can, I'll have someone in Israel mail you the invitation—like we got. I bet by next year you'll all be in Jerusalem."

Misha screamed and ran out of the apartment.

"What's wrong?" asked Marina in a frightened voice.

Mrs. Pasternack had tears in her eyes. "Today, we learned that we have been rejected for the fourth time. It's been going on for over two years."

"Oh, no!" said Marina, who was trying to hold back her own tears. "Once we are out of Odessa, there must be some way we can help you. My parents will know. They're very smart."

"Of course!" agreed Uncle Mordecai, who wanted to sound hopeful for his niece. He smiled one of those beautiful Pasternack grins. When Marina saw it, the lump in her throat hurt her even more.

9

Thirty Days

The moment Marina left for Misha's, Vasily announced he was going down to see the building manager.

"Do you think he'll be difficult?" asked Klara.

"Probably. But we'll come to terms." Mr. Birger reached into his back pocket and checked for his wallet.

"Be careful, darling."

Mr. Kopitch, the building manager, resided on the second floor. Vasily knocked on his apartment door. When there was no answer, he banged harder.

"Is there a problem, Comrade Birger?"

Vasily looked behind him and saw the manager coming up the steps.

"Not a problem, but we need to talk."

"Yes?"

Vasily stepped closer to the man and whispered, "My family and I have just received permission for exit visas to Israel. We need a signed *spravka* from you for OVIR."

Mr. Kopitch scratched his head. "I'm not quite sure what you mean."

Mr. Birger could not believe that a building manager would be so uninformed about such matters, but he remained calm.

"Sir," he began patiently, "in order for us to receive the visas, I must present a notice from you stating that I owe you no money and that I am returning the apartment in satisfactory condition."

"You don't say," the building manager remarked. "Well, I guess I'll have to inspect your place."

"Of course," agreed Vasily. "When would it be convenient for you?"

"Oh, my days are hectic," groaned Kopitch. "It will be at least three or four weeks. I'll put you down on my list and get back to you."

Vasily had anticipated such a response and slowly extended his right arm. His hand was closed, but for an instant he loosened his grip so that the building manager could see what he was holding. "I would be so appreciative if you would stop by now. I'm sure it would only take a few moments."

Mr. Kopitch stared at Vasily's fist. He grinned and put out his own right arm. As the two men shook hands, rubles passed from one palm to another. "I guess I do have a free moment," muttered the building manager as he stuffed the money into his pocket. "Of course, you understand that I refuse to sign any *spravka* unless your apartment is in perfect order."

"Naturally," replied Mr. Birger. "But I'm sure we'll be able to resolve any differences."

"I'm sure," laughed the building manager, and he followed Vasily up the stairs.

Mr. Kopitch surveyed the premises with a critical eye. It was obvious no repairs were needed. Finally, he admitted, "I don't see too many flaws. Still, this place must be freshly painted before the new tenants can take occupancy. You get the work done, and I'll sign your *spravka.*"

Klara was about to speak out, but Vasily's expression silenced her.

"We suspected that some painting might be necessary," he agreed, "but it is a rather hectic time for us. Perhaps, if I pay you for the paint and a little extra for the labor, you can take care of it?"

The manager grinned. "You're a shrewd one, Comrade Birger. Of course, all you Jews have smart heads for business." He howled with laughter.

Vasily reached into his back pocket for his wallet. As

he went to open it, he remembered, "Oh, the *spravka!*"

Quickly, Klara handed a pen and the notice to the building manager. Mr. Kopitch made a face as he scribbled his initials at the bottom of the paper.

"My money!" he said. Vasily handed him more rubles, and Kopitch made a hasty exit.

"What a thief!" whispered Mrs. Birger after she heard the door slam. "He'll never use that money to paint this apartment. Besides, we just painted last September."

"Who cares?" declared Vasily as he held the *spravka* high in the air. Suddenly, he threw his arms around his wife and they began to waltz around the room. They were still hugging and laughing when Marina entered. Both were so pleased about the day's events, they did not notice Marina's glum expression.

"So? Are you and Misha friends again?" teased Mrs. Birger as she pulled away from her husband's embrace.

"I don't know," Marina mumbled. Then she explained what had happened downstairs. "I wouldn't blame him if he hates me more," she concluded.

"It's tragic," Mr. Birger said solemnly. "They're such fine people."

"But what can we do, Papa? There must be something we can do!"

"Nothing," Marina's father sighed.

"Perhaps you can give something to Misha," Mrs. Birger said, "something special that will remind him you care."

* * *

Besides the *spravka* from Mr. Kopitch, the Birgers needed other notices for OVIR. Vasily had no difficulties obtaining the *spravkas* from the University. All he had to do was make copies of his and Klara's diplomas and submit the authentic ones to the University. In return, the school agreed to sign the notices for OVIR. But the telephone company was a different story.

"I'm sorry," the clerk said to Klara. "We only do these forms from nine A.M. to nine thirty A.M. It's now nine thirty-two."

The next day Vasily returned with Klara at 9:00 A.M.

"Oh, your wife wasn't paying attention," the clerk snickered. "Those times were for yesterday. Today, we don't even look at *spravkas*. We're too busy with much more important matters. Try next Tuesday."

"What time?" snapped Vasily.

"Well, if you're going to act like that!" said the clerk in a huff.

"Please," Klara said apologetically, "my husband did not mean to sound so impatient. What time do you recommend we be down here?"

"Between nine and nine thirty A.M.," hollered the clerk. "Good day, Madam!" The clerk jerked his head back and pointed to the exit.

OVIR also required a citizen's workbook. All Russians were issued a book as soon as they entered the work force. Unlike a personal résumé, an individual had no control over what was documented in these records. Mr. Anatassy still had Klara's and Vasily's at the hospital.

"Yes?" said the receptionist outside Mr. Anatassy's office. She acted as if Vasily were a stranger.

"I'd like to see Mr. Anatassy, please."

"He's busy."

"You could at least tell him I'm here."

"Take a seat."

Mr. Birger sat there for two hours. When Mr. Anatassy finally appeared at his door, he gasped at seeing Vasily in the waiting area. The receptionist had never announced his arrival.

"Why are you here?" Anatassy asked gruffly. "I thought I made it clear how the hospital feels about people like you." He spoke loud enough so that the receptionist could hear him.

"Klara and I have been granted permission to go to Israel. We need our workbooks."

Mr. Birger expected a friendlier reception once they were alone inside the office, but Mr. Anatassy remained very aloof. He unlocked his file and took out Klara's and Vasily's books. He dated them and signed his name.

"Thank you," Mr. Birger said as he reached out for them. He waited a moment, hoping his old boss would say something more.

"Is there anything else?" Mr. Anatassy inquired.

"I guess not," Vasily sighed. He turned and started toward the door. Suddenly, he heard his name.

"Vasily! You forgot this!"

Mr. Birger stopped. Mr. Anatassy was at his side and

slipped a piece of paper into his coat pocket. "You always were dropping things," he muttered.

Vasily looked down at his pocket and then at Mr. Anatassy. Both men smiled and silently said their good-bys.

"So?" asked Klara, who had been waiting anxiously all morning.

Mr. Birger held out the two workbooks. Then he reached into his pocket for the slip of paper.

"What's that?" Klara asked.

"A good-by note from Mr. Anatassy."

After Klara had read the few sentences, she muttered to herself, "How could I have doubted him?" Then she said to Vasily, "I'll be sure to pack this."

Without any warning, Vasily grabbed the slip and ripped it into tiny bits.

"What are you doing?" asked Klara.

"This is no time for sentiment!" he scolded.

"But it's just well wishes from an old colleague," she argued. "What harm could it do?"

"Plenty. Just remember Brest! The customs official there will search everything we own before he lets us pass. What if he says this note is a secret code?"

The mention of Brest made Mrs. Birger think of all the obstacles still ahead of them. She quickly picked up the pieces of paper and flushed them down the toilet.

Marina had her own special appointment that day.

"I'm ve-ve-very sorry, Mr. Fyodorov," Marina stuttered. "I-I-I won't be able to participate in the storytell-ing contest."

It was very warm inside the tiny office, and as Ma-rina stood at attention in front of the obese principal, she could feel beads of sweat on her forehead and un-derneath her collar.

"Why not?" he demanded. When she tried to an-swer, her speech was barely audible.

"Talk up!" he said.

Marina took a deep breath and started again. "My parents and I have been granted exit visas for Israel. We leave in less than a month."

The principal pounded his fist. "You assured me your parents had no intention of applying for a visa."

"It was true then."

Mr. Fyodorov stood up and leaned his bulging mid-dle over the desk. "How can I believe anything you say? Get out of my sight!"

Marina was so scared, she did not notice a chair and tripped. She stumbled into a tall man just entering the office.

"Ouch!" he cried.

Marina jumped back. "Excuse me," she said without looking up at him.

"You clumsy child!" screamed Fyodorov. "Get back to your classroom." He motioned to the man, "Come in, Boris." As Marina walked by, she caught a glimpse of the stranger. It was the same KGB official who had searched her apartment.

Once alone, the tall man said, "That's the one, isn't it?"

Mr. Fyodorov smiled and nodded. "By the way, thank you. They leave in less than a month. Of course, I didn't let on." The rotund educator started snickering. "Can you imagine what those Jews would say if they knew KGB had actually helped them?"

"Hey! I didn't do it for any Jew! It's strictly business. I owed you a favor, and you were just lucky that someone in the right place owed me one. So those Jews got their visas one, two, three. Seems to me you could have just thrown her out of the contest."

"I could have, but I didn't want anyone pointing the finger at me. Her story was too good to ignore, but I knew sooner or later sponsoring a Jew would cause trouble. This way she's out of my hair, and I can point the finger at someone else." The men enjoyed a good laugh together.

An hour later, Mrs. Krezshnovskaya sat in Fyodorov's office. When the principal told her the news, the social studies teacher gasped.

"You're fortunate I'm not so cold-hearted," he said. "Do you realize your story champion comes from a family of traitors? We all could have been penalized."

Mrs. Krezshnovskaya apologized over and over again. When she returned to her classroom, her beady eyes scanned the room for Marina. "Where is she? Where is Marina Birger?"

"She left," Shura called out. "I watched her leave after Mr. Shatz's class."

Misha, too, had watched Marina run out the front entrance and wondered what had happened.

"Is Marina all right?" Misha asked Mr. Birger outside the door.

"Of course," said Mr. Birger. "Come in."

The children had not spoken since that night Marina had told the Pasternacks she would be leaving Odessa. She assumed Misha was avoiding her because he was still angry. The truth was that he was too embarrassed to apologize for his outburst. This afternoon, however, he was worried about her.

"Hi!" he said, feeling awkward. "Why did you run out of school in the middle of the day? Krezshnovskaya was asking for you."

"I'm sure she was," Marina answered sarcastically.

"I don't understand."

"I told Mr. Fyodorov I would not be in the finals." Marina repeated the principal's comments.

"Marina won't be returning to that school," Mrs. Birger stated emphatically. "Anyway, we can use her help."

"Can you imagine what the kids will call me? I can already hear Shura's big mouth."

"Don't worry," said Misha. "I won't let them criticize you."

Marina smiled.

"Hey," the boy said quickly. "I'm sorry about the other night. Come down later, and tell me all about your plans." He was out of the apartment before anyone could say a word.

At dinner, Mrs. Birger started shaking her head. "Marina, you can't start running in and out of the Pasternack place again. It's too dangerous. And I don't want Misha here, either. The authorities can still revoke the decision, and then what?"

"Please, Mama, please!" pleaded Marina. "Just one last time, and I'll never go there again. Please!"

Marina promised to stay no more than fifteen minutes. As she walked down the stairway, she clutched to her chest a present for Misha. She saw Mrs. Pasternack standing outside her apartment door. The woman was about to light up a cigarette but then noticed Marina.

"Hello. You're a bit earlier than we expected."

"I can't stay very long, Mrs. Pasternack. May I go in?"

Ina nervously slipped the pack of cigarettes into her pocket and put her hand on the doorknob. "You stay here for a moment. I'll just make sure Uncle Mordecai is up to visitors right now."

Marina had not expected this response and stood there worried she would never have her last visit. While she anxiously waited for the door to reopen, Mrs. Stakavitzkaya stepped out into the hallway.

"I thought I heard voices. What are you doing here?"

146 · *MONDAY IN ODESSA*

"Waiting for Misha."

"Haven't I warned you and your family enough times?" snarled the fat gossip. "Those people in there are lawbreakers. I'm sure the authorities are watching them."

Marina wanted to ask the woman how she knew so much about the "authorities," but just then Misha opened the door.

"Why did I have to wait?" whispered Marina, once she was safely inside the foyer.

"Sorry. We were studying."

Marina instinctively knew he was referring to something "Judaic," which, of course, meant illegal. "After all that has happened?" she asked.

"We're more careful," he assured her. "Mother stands outside and smokes a cigarette. That way she can warn us."

"I didn't think your mother smoked."

"She doesn't, really," admitted Misha. "It's just an excuse for her to be meandering outside the door. She tells everyone that Uncle Mordecai objects to the smoke in the apartment."

Marina felt a chill go through her as she thought of the vicious woman across the hall, waiting and watching.

"I brought you a present," she said, wanting to change the subject.

"Really? What?" Misha glanced at the folder.

"No! You can't look until I leave," teased Marina,

and then she walked in to say good evening to Uncle Mordecai.

The moment Marina had left, Misha opened the folder. "I can't believe this," he hollered. "She gave me her story! 'A Heart of Courage'!" He immediately sat down by his uncle's side and read the manuscript aloud. "Isn't it wonderful?" he asked at the end.

"Yes," agreed Uncle Mordecai. "I shall miss that delightful child. Then he put his arm around his nephew and whispered, "You must give her something, too."

Besides Misha, Marina had one other person she wished to see before leaving Odessa. That person was Ivan Chernetzky at the music conservatory. In the last two months he had continued to substitute at the school, and he and Marina had become good friends. Every morning he would tease her about their first meeting. The day she came to say good-by, he greeted her with his standard line.

"I see you remembered, today."

"Come on," Marina whined. "You know I only made the mistake once, and it really wasn't my fault."

"Tsk, tsk, tsk. I usually get at least a giggle from you. I must be losing my touch."

"It's not you," Marina said quietly. "I'm just not in a giggly mood."

"I hope you're in a Chopin mood," he said and winked.

Marina paused for a moment and then replied, "You probably won't want to have a lesson with me today. I've come to say good-by."

"Good-by?" He looked at her as if he had not heard correctly. "How can you give up your music studies? You're very talented, Marina." Suddenly, he jumped up from his seat. "I must talk to your parents at once."

"You don't understand," pleaded Marina. "I'm not quitting the piano. I'm leaving. I'm leaving for Israel with my parents. We go in a few weeks."

Marina knew very well that Ivan was not Jewish, but she had always assumed from his friendly manner that he was not an anti-Semite. His silence, however, scared her, and suddenly she regretted her decision to see him.

"I'm shocked," he whispered.

Marina had not yet unpacked her music and stepped away from him. "I-I just th-thought," she stammered, "that you'd like to say good-by."

"Oh, Marina, of course!" Then he whispered again, "What a lucky girl you are!"

Marina began to laugh nervously. "I thought you were angry."

"Angry? No! A little jealous, perhaps."

"But you're not a Jew. Why would you be jealous?"

"My career is shaped by the State. If I could leave, I could shape my own destiny."

Marina stared up at the young man. "I never knew you thought about such things."

"And that's how it must be. Now, let's hear you play."

Marina's lesson extended past the usual hour. By the time she returned home, the afternoon children were congregating on the school steps. She looked straight ahead to avoid eye contact with any familiar faces. Still, Shura saw her and shouted out her name. Marina pretended not to hear and walked into her building. But Shura darted across the street and followed Marina into the lobby.

"Hey! Aren't you coming to school today?"

"No," Marina answered bluntly.

"Why not? You don't look sick."

"I'm not."

"So what is it?" nagged Shura. "You can't stay home just because you feel like it. Especially you. You're a model for the whole school."

"Some model!" piped in a voice from the back corner. Sitting there with her long knitting needles was Mrs. Stakavitzkaya.

"Well, she is!" insisted Shura. "You'll be reading about her in the newspaper this summer."

"I doubt it!" cackled the woman.

Marina gestured for Shura to keep quiet, but the classmate did not take the hint.

"Don't listen to her, Marina. She's just an old busybody." Shura purposely did not lower her voice.

"Watch your tongue, young lady," screamed Mrs. Stakavitzkaya.

Marina went to pull Shura toward the doorway, but before she could make her move, the insolent child mimicked, "You watch it, lady!" Then she stuck out her tongue and burst into a fit of giggles.

Marina pressed her own two lips together in an attempt to maintain a serious expression, but Shura's laughter was contagious.

Mrs. Stakavitzkaya shook her finger at Shura. "Laugh all you like, you shameful girl. You'll be crying plenty after your mother finds out you play with traitors. Mr. Kopitch told everybody, Marina."

The laughter stopped. "What does she mean?" Shura demanded. "Who's Kopitch?"

"He's just the building manager," Marina said quickly. "Come on. School will start soon." Once again she tried to pull Shura toward the door.

"Your girlfriend's going to Israel," yelled Mrs. Stakavitzkaya. "Her family leaves in less than a month."

"But the storytelling contest," cried Shura. "You can't go anywhere."

"I had to forfeit it," Marina whispered. "You wouldn't understand," she started up the stairway.

"I understand just fine," Shura shouted after her. "You better not come back to school." Then she began chanting, "Traitor, traitor, traitor! That's why we all hate her." Marina raced up the steps, covering her ears.

* * *

After ten days of waiting and lines and verbal abuse, Vasily was able to return to OVIR with all the necessary papers. The secretary examined each document.

"Okay," she finally said. "I see no problems. Of course, I need the registration fee for each applicant."

Mr. Birger counted out 120 rubles—40 per person.

"Do I receive the visas from you?"

"No. At the bank. After you pay the full amount."

Vasily already knew that for each of them he would have to deposit 860 rubles, or 2,580 rubles in all. The sum represented a huge chunk of their savings. If for any reason they did not leave the country, the Birgers would have no work and little money.

Although he now had the visas in his possession, the documents still were not valid. During the next six days, he traveled alone to Kiev and Moscow. At the OVIR in Kiev, he waited almost two days until someone finally stamped his visas, the family's birth certificates, his and Klara's marriage license, and the copies of their University diplomas. These family records were to be submitted at the Foreign Department in Moscow.

"Eventually, all these papers should be returned to you—wherever you are," a cocky clerk told Mr. Birger. Vasily, however, did not expect to see the records again.

After the Foreign Department, Mr. Birger stood in lines at the Polish, Czech, and Austrian embassies. Each had to indicate with an official stamp that the Birger family would be allowed to cross its borders.

His last stop in Moscow was the bank. Vasily showed the teller at the window his two exit visas. Because Marina was underage, her name was included on Klara's.

"Please," he said, "I need to change my rubles for American dollars." He then placed 270 rubles on the counter.

"Hey, mister, you can't do that. You'll never get away with it."

"But it's my money," he protested.

"Sure. For now. But the law states that a Jew cannot take more than the equivalent of 90 rubles out of the country."

Vasily still looked perplexed. "So what's the problem?"

"No problem for me, but you've got a big one. Ninety and ninety equals one hundred and eighty."

Vasily showed him Klara's visa again and pointed to Marina's name.

"I'm not sure if children count," mumbled the embarrassed clerk, but he still pushed the American dollars through the window.

Vasily came home to a living room of boxes and suitcases. While he had been away, Klara had arranged for the piano, china cabinet, bookcase, plus three large boxes of books, silver, china, and crystal, to be shipped to an address in Jerusalem. The rest she planned to sell or give to neighbors in the building.

When Marina had asked about the phony address, Klara assured her they would have no problems. "Nothing goes directly," she explained. "All shipments first stop in Vienna. When we get there, we'll have it corrected."

All that had to be done now was to purchase three train tickets. The morning after he returned from Moscow, Vasily took the trolley downtown to the hotel restricted for foreign guests. He presented his exit visas to a female clerk at the transportation counter.

"Please, Comrade," he said courteously. "I need three tickets for Vienna."

The woman glared at him. "How dare you stand there with exit visas and call me 'Comrade'?"

"Madam, I meant no offense. Now, please, about the tickets?"

"Sorry. We've got nothing for eighteen days," she answered curtly.

"But it must be sooner or our visas will expire."

"That's your headache, mister," she replied with a yawn.

"Please," begged Vasily.

"Try later in the week. Who knows? Maybe we'll have a cancellation."

The next three nights Vasily tossed and turned in bed, worried that his worst fear was about to become a reality. Although Klara suspected something was upsetting her husband, neither she nor Marina was aware of the problem. He had told them the tickets would be issued in four days.

Four days later he returned to the hotel and spoke to a different woman. "There's plenty of room next week," she said. "I don't know where you heard your information, but if you have the money, I've got the tickets."

Without another word, Vasily put his 84 rubles down on the counter.

The tickets were stamped June 2. When Marina saw the dated stubs, she cried, "Mama! Mama! I hope you didn't pack the camera yet. I need it. I need it now."

"Sh, Marina," Mrs. Birger whispered. "Keep your voice down."

"Please," she said more quietly. "I want to take pictures of the neighborhood."

"It's in the small compartment of the red-leather suitcase. I think there are eight more pictures on the roll."

Until that moment Marina had not thought of taking pictures of her school, the movie house, the supermarket, or the neighborhood street vendors. In the past they had all seemed so ordinary. She even walked that long stretch from the conservatory down to the hospital. She thought her parents would especially like those photographs.

Marina returned home expecting to take one last snapshot. She sat by her window and waited for the school dismissal. When she saw Misha walk out of the main entrance, she ran down the stairs.

"Smile!" she shouted as he stepped up on the curb.

Misha looked up and saw Marina focusing the camera. He made a silly face.

"No! Not like that. Look nice."

Misha flashed that smile she loved so much, and Marina clicked instantly.

"Perfect!" she said, and turned to go into the building.

"Hey! What's your rush?" Misha yelled after her. The children had spoken very little since Marina had given him "A Heart of Courage." "I've got some juicy stories about Krezshnovskaya," he said, trying to arouse her curiosity.

Marina saw Mrs. Stakavitzkaya coming up the street. "I'd better go."

Misha grabbed her arm. "When do you leave?"

"Tuesday night. Our train pulls out at ten."

They stood with their eight suitcases and waited for the taxi. Some of the tenants passing through the lobby stopped to wish the Birgers success in their new life, but not Mrs. Stakavitzkaya.

"I'm really surprised," she said to Mr. and Mrs. Birger. "I always thought you were smart. Don't you know those trains are searched day and night? What are you people going to do without passports? You don't even have a country to call your own. See how much an exit visa helps you if there's trouble." She would have continued to harass them, but the cab driver appeared at the door.

As they pulled away, Marina whispered, "Was what she said true?"

"Don't think about it," replied Mrs. Birger. "It will be all right." Marina pressed her face against the window and looked out at the dark buildings.

To the Birgers' surprise, Misha and his mother were waiting for them at the train station.

"I know we said our good-bys last night, but Uncle Mordecai insisted we see you off properly," explained Mrs. Pasternack.

"Besides," Misha said, "I bought a present for Marina today. I just got it this morning." He handed her a wrapped package.

"What is it?" Marina asked excitedly. She had hoped Misha would give her something.

"Oh, no," the boy laughed. "You'll have to wait until you're on the train."

Just then the voice over the loudspeaker made the boarding announcement. Marina quickly slipped the package into her tote bag.

Until now the children had been too self-conscious to hug one another, but tonight, without any warning, Misha threw his arms around Marina and squeezed her with all his might. He released her only when the voice repeated the announcement. The family hurried onto the train. Misha and his mother stood at the track and continued to wave until the train was out of sight.

Once she was settled in her compartment, Marina unwrapped her surprise. It was an anthology of fairy tales, very similar to the one Misha's father had bought for him. Inside the cover jacket the boy had written, "To my favorite storyteller." The present made Marina even sadder, and she put it back into her tote bag.

The train arrived in Kiev the next morning at nine and was not scheduled to depart until 5:00 P.M. The family spent the day in the city, but no one had much enthusiasm for sightseeing. Marina was sad and tired, and her parents were nervous. Their next stop was Brest.

It was 5:00 A.M. when the conductor announced Brest. The trainload of passengers lined up with their baggage in a small stationhouse. Everyone was surprised to see only one customs official.

Marina watched with horror as the woman emptied out whole suitcases and threw people's underwear around the room. Her task was to look for illegal drugs, weapons, or documents, but the official often abused her authority. The Birgers saw her confiscate jewelry, furs, and silver.

When it was their turn, the woman glanced at Klara's hands. "You can't take that with you," she said and pointed to Klara's gold ring.

"But that's my wedding band."

The official held out her palm, waiting for Mrs. Birger to remove her ring. Vasily ordered his wife to take it off immediately.

The official then grabbed the red suitcase and unzipped the smaller pouch where Marina had repacked her camera.

"No, no, no!" the inspector teased and held the camera high in the air.

"But you can't take that!" screamed Marina. The roll of undeveloped pictures was still inside the camera.

The woman's laughter stopped. "Hush your daughter, or I won't let any of you pass. Let me see your papers."

As Mr. Birger reached into his briefcase for the exit visas, a second customs official walked into the station. His uniform was wrinkled and his face unshaven.

"Where have you been, you lazy oaf. How am I supposed to take care of all these people myself?"

"Please, I had a rough night. Just tell me where you want me to start."

"Right here," and suddenly she shoved Marina's camera into the man's hand. "Just make sure you're faster than yesterday, or I'll report I saw you drinking on the job." The woman then went to the back of the room.

The disheveled inspector put the camera down and quickly opened all eight suitcases. He glanced inside each one. "You're okay," he grunted.

While her parents closed their bags, Marina went

over to the man and tapped him on the shoulder. She made sure the female official was not watching.

"May I take my camera now?" she asked sweetly.

The guard had forgotten about the camera. Quickly he opened it, ripped out the film, and exposed the undeveloped roll to the light. "You can take it now," he muttered and handed her the camera. The film he tossed on the floor.

Marina stooped over to pick up the roll. Although she knew it was unlikely, she hoped a few pictures could be saved—especially the one of Misha.

"Hey, Miss," the guard said. "That film's no good. Dump it!" His arm was stretched out, and he was pointing to something behind her. Marina turned around and saw the trash can.

The train left Brest at 12:30 P.M. An hour later it crossed into Poland and stopped. Soldiers boarded the cars, demanding to see passports and visas. Everyone sat quietly as the stern Poles paced up and down the corridors. After the men were gone, passengers breathed easier and chatted.

Marina struck up a conversation with a set of twelve-year-old twins from Kiev. They, too, said they were moving to Israel, but Marina wondered if, like herself, their final destination was America. Even on the train, no one dared to mention the United States or Canada. As friendly as everybody seemed, strangers could not be trusted.

At 4:00 P.M. they stopped in Warsaw, and their railroad car was attached to a new train named the War-saw-Paris.

Marina was exhausted from the last two days of travel and fell asleep easily that night. She did not know how long she had been asleep when she heard loud voices in the corridor. She peeked through her door and saw soldiers examining visas. Her parents had warned her that the train would stop many times before Vienna.

Marina was still awake the second time the engines stopped. A new group of soldiers boarded. They wore different uniforms, and their language sounded different from the Polish she had heard all day. Marina guessed that they had just crossed into Czechoslovakia. Peeking through the door again, she watched her father present the visas. He pointed to Marina's compartment to identify his child.

Marina hurried back to her bed before the young soldier pushed open her door. He found her huddled underneath a blanket. Then he noticed her tote bag at the foot of her berth. He grabbed it and turned it upside down. Everything fell to the floor. He picked up the anthology.

"Fairy tales," Marina said nervously. "Stories for children." She spoke slowly and used motions, believing the soldier could not understand her.

"Don't insult me!" he hollered in perfect Russian. He began to flip through the pages and Marina thought of the night the two KGB men had searched the apartment.

"What's this?" he asked and pointed to a handwritten paper taped inside the book. Marina looked at it and saw Misha's writing.

"Just a story. I won a school contest for it. I figured it would be safe in there," she lied. "Do you want to hear it?"

"A school contest?" the soldier sneered. "Don't waste my time," and he threw the book on the floor. Marina did not budge until she was sure all the guards were off the train. Once she heard the engines start again, she scurried out of her berth and picked up the anthology. After a few seconds, she found Misha's "real" present. Word for word, he had copied Uncle Mordecai's "Queen Esther" manuscript and had taped it to the pages of a fairy tale—just like he had done with his own in Odessa. Settled in her berth again, she read the story, closed the book, and closed her eyes.

The train stopped for soldiers twice more. The last time, everyone applauded for the men. These were the guards hired by the Jewish immigration agencies, HIAS and SACHNUT. Their job was to protect Soviet Jews once they had crossed the border into Austria.

"It's like coming to paradise," Klara and Vasily kept repeating as they looked out at the vibrant city of Vienna. Mrs. Birger recalled her sister, Lena, raving in her letters about color television in the West. She had described a Russian's life as changing from "black and white" to "living color."

"I hoped it would be like this," exclaimed Marina. "It's just like being in *The Sound of Music.*" Other people on the train heard the comment and agreed. Everyone laughed and hugged and kissed and cried.

As Marina was stepping off the train, she heard her father say again, "Yes. Yes. It's just like paradise." Then she accidentally stumbled and fell to the ground. In seconds, a handsome officer from SACHNUT was by her side. He extended his hand and smiled.

Marina looked up at him. His boyish grin made her think of Misha.

"No, Papa," she muttered to herself. "It's not quite paradise."

A Final Word

Like Marina Birger, my dear friend, Marina Khait, slept on a sofa bed by her parents' side in a tiny one-room apartment. She, too, wore the soft slippers at school. She, too, carried old newspapers in her tote bag for grocery shopping. It was from Ms. Khait's detailed account of her life in Odessa that I created the setting for *Monday in Odessa*. I thank my friend for all her guidance, patience, and support.

I also wish to express my gratitude to Marina's father, Alexander Khait, who so vividly described for me the long and difficult application process, the frantic "thirty days," and the final train ride to freedom.

The Khait family left Odessa in 1973, when 34,733 Jews were permitted to leave the Soviet Union. The number surged to 51,320 in 1979. Since then, the figure has declined dramatically. In 1984, emigration dropped to only 896. This is not to say, however, that Jews no longer wish to leave the Soviet Union. It has been estimated that more than 350,000 Soviet Jews have taken preliminary steps in the emigration process, and that 20,000 of those Jews have been denied their exit visas.